PRIVATE ACTS

DELANEY DIAMOND

GARDEN AVENUE PRESS

Private Acts by Delaney Diamond

Copyright © 2012, Delaney Diamond

Garden Avenue Press

Atlanta, GA

ISBN: 978-0-9852838-9-6 (Ebook edition)

ISBN: 978-1-940636-51-1 (Paperback edition)

CHAPTER 1

*I*t was good to be back.

Miguel Delgado inhaled deeply, appreciating the familiar sounds and smells of his birthplace in the highlands of Ecuador. After the street vendor handed him the small bag filled with *chifles*, he paid her and walked away. He popped one into his mouth, enjoying the crunch of the thinly sliced fried bananas. They were one of the things he'd missed during his last sojourn to the States. After he arrived earlier today, he took a short nap before deciding to venture out.

He turned down a side street toward the bar owned by his friend, Seth, a former military man from Texas who'd first visited Cuenca over ten years ago. He'd met and fallen in love with a Cuencaran, chucked his life in the States, and opened Seth's Bar for other transplants like himself. Expats from the English-speaking countries of the United States, Canada, and Britain frequented the spot.

Monday nights were rowdy and as busy as weekend nights because it was Karaoke Night. As a form of appreciation, customers donated cash, all of which was placed in a jar as prize money for the most popular singers.

Miguel stood inside the door for a moment and watched as another wannabe singer walked awkwardly back and forth across the small stage, singing a fifties song in the worst falsetto he'd ever heard. He couldn't understand why anyone would stand up on a stage and put the spotlight on themselves in that way. It wasn't worth the money. To think, people in bars around the world sang karaoke for *free*.

He walked up to the bar, and after he caught his friend's eye, shook his head. "How can you put up with this noise?" He gestured toward the stage.

Seth laughed, grabbing his hand over the bar and shaking it vigorously. "After ten years, I don't even hear them anymore." Before Miguel could ask, Seth opened an Ecuadorian beer and set it on the polished wood in front of him.

He tipped the bottle in thanks and took a swallow.

"So how was Miami?" Seth asked.

"The same. I'm glad to be back."

The tension between him and his mother had mounted to an unpleasant level, but the meeting with his art agent had gone well. Several of his sculptures had sold above the asking price with buyers clamoring for more.

"Yeah, I'm glad I left that rat race. There's no place like Cuenca, am I right?"

"No place like it," Miguel agreed. He came to the realization a long time ago and never missed the hustle and bustle of larger cities when he was home.

"What about Miguelito?" Seth asked. He always referred to Miguel's eleven-year-old brother as "little Miguel" because of how much they looked alike, despite having different fathers.

Miguel dropped onto one of the bar stools and raked his fingers through his hair. Aarón had sulked in his room from the moment he arrived, but any attempts he made to find out what was wrong had met with resistance. The harder he pushed, the more withdrawn his brother became. His mother hadn't been any help, claiming nothing was wrong. But he knew she didn't see it because she chose not to. She would rather cater to the needs of her latest lover than acknowledge any problems in the relationship between her and Aarón.

"I know he's unhappy, but he won't talk to me."

"He will when he's ready," Seth said with confidence as he wiped down the bar. "Think of yourself at that age."

"I barely remember it."

In truth, he remembered eleven quite well, but he wished he didn't. Twenty years ago he'd been a bitter, angry youth, and it hadn't been a pleasant period in his life. He hoped his brother didn't experience the same turmoil he had.

In addition to meeting with his art agent, the visit to Miami had been meant to get his brother to open up to him, but it seemed he'd clammed up even more. He would have to endure his brother's stoicism until he felt ready to talk, but he would not give up.

The sound of applause and cheers from the crowd caught his attention. The first performer had left the stage, and a new performer, a woman, had taken his place. She was the reason the crowd had gone wild. She tapped the microphone to check the acoustics and smiled at the audience. With her dark skin, she stood out from the other patrons of a paler complexion. Outside of the small number of Afro-Ecuadorians in the country, it was unusual to see Blacks in town.

"*Hola amigos!*" she said, resulting in an enthusiastic response of hollering and whistling from the crowd. She even received an enthusiastic greeting from the women.

"Who is she?"

"*That* is Samirah Jamison."

Miguel glanced at his friend, who stood staring at the stage with his beefy arms crossed over his chest and a goofy smile on his face. His gaze slid back to the stage. Who was this woman that she warranted such a reception from the entire bar?

3

She was attractive, he admitted, with long black hair parted in the middle and allowed to tumble into waves past her shoulders, brushing each cheek to frame her face. In fact, she looked like a piece of art. His artist eyes took a slow tour of her body, taking in each line and curve. The brightly-colored fitted shirt dipped to a vee over her abundant breasts. The shirt tucked into the waistband of a pair of denim, painted-on white capris that left little to the imagination and accentuated the hourglass narrowness of her waistline.

His eyes made their way back up to her face and the brilliant smile she wielded like a weapon at her admirers. She must be a good singer to elicit such adoration. At least he thought so until she started singing her rendition of "I Will Survive" by Gloria Gaynor.

At first he couldn't believe how bad she was, but twenty-five seconds in the song picked up tempo, and so did she. The crowd started clapping when she pulled the mike from the stand and began to dance around the stage. She made eye contact with patrons at the first few tables, leaning forward to sing to individuals in the audience.

Silver hoops peeked between the strands of her thick hair and caught the light as she moved her body, gyrating her hips and sashaying across the stage while enthusiastically singing off key. She was obviously enjoying herself, holding her head up high and waving her hands with attitude about how she would survive.

Miguel found himself enthralled like everyone else, unable to take his eyes off of her. What she lacked in singing ability, she more than made up for in her performance. At one point, she turned her back to the audience and looked over her shoulder, crooning into the microphone with one hand on her swaying hips and a seductive smile on her lips. His body reacted to her movements. His groin muscles contracted as she teased him and every red-blooded man in the place into noticing her generous backside—and imagining doing all sorts of salacious things to it.

Miguel picked up his beer and took a sip to wet his suddenly dry tongue. As she neared the end of the song, she incorporated a shimmy, moving her body in a snakelike, provocative manner.

She stopped for a moment to lift her right hand in the air to hit a particularly difficult note—which she didn't hit. As the song ended, her arm reached for the ceiling, and her head fell back as she became lost in the music. She held the pose for long seconds as the customers jumped to their feet and clapped.

She hadn't removed an item of clothing, but her performance resulted in the same reaction as a strip tease. Miguel remained frozen, his eyes riveted on the smooth column of her throat and the tight arch of her body. An uncomfortable, tightening sensation spread across his chest, and he released his suspended breath.

"*That* is Samirah," Seth yelled over the noise of thunderous applause he joined in with everyone else.

Samirah took a deep bow, allowing her hair to fall forward in a shiny black sheath before standing upright to descend the stairs with the help of one of the male patrons. She'd cast a spell over the entire crowd. Men and women alike gave her high fives as she made her way back to the bar. She appeared to be the kind of woman who got noticed wherever she went, and she was the kind of woman who enjoyed being noticed. It was evident in the confident way she glided through the tables, shoulders thrown back and head held high.

She didn't acknowledge Miguel's presence when she bounced up and slapped her palms on top of the bar.

"What will it be, gorgeous?" Seth asked. Miguel noticed the unmistakable lowering of his friend's voice.

Samirah tucked her hair behind her left ear, giving Miguel a good view of her delicate features—a small ear, the roundness of her chin, and a mouth with a plump lower lip. With the soft curve of her luscious mouth, he got the impression she laughed often.

"Ginger ale, but only a little bit of ice." She reached toward the pocket of her pants.

"Hey, hey!" Seth chided her. "You know your money's no good here." He added two cubes of ice to the glass.

"Seth, you can't continue to let me drink for free." She leaned forward and whispered, "The other customers will get mad."

He set the filled glass on the counter and dropped in a straw, leaning toward her. "I've got you covered, gorgeous."

Miguel slipped another *chifle* into his mouth as he watched the exchange. His neck muscles grew taut, and he crunched down much harder than normal. Had Seth forgotten he was happily married? That was the second time he'd called her gorgeous, and Miguel felt an unnatural elevation in his temperature. His friend's flirtations irritated him. Maybe he needed to be reminded he had a damn wife at home.

"You're too good to me." She blew him a kiss and picked up the glass.

When Seth walked away to take care of another customer, she took a sip. Then she lifted her eyes to his face, and for a moment he felt like he'd been clobbered in the chest. The curiosity in her dark brown eyes played out in her next words.

"*¿Te conozco?*"

He couldn't blame her for asking, considering he'd been staring at her since she walked up. Her Spanish pronunciation was good, but she definitely had an accent, and he guessed her to be from either Canada or the United States. "I speak English," he replied. "And no, you don't know me."

He caught a few *chifles* between his fingers and popped them into his mouth.

* * *

SAMIRAH WAS USED to getting attention. In fact, she thrived on it because, as the youngest of three, she'd sometimes felt overshadowed by the perfection of her older brother and sister. But something about this man's attention unnerved her. He looked like he wanted to pop her in his mouth the way he had the savory snack.

She'd never seen him in the bar before, which was no surprise, since this was a gringo bar. He presented a feast for the eyes. A scar above his left eye sliced through his dark brow. The pale slice of fibrous tissue, rather than detracting from his physical appearance, served to enhance it by adding a dangerous edge to his features. The light blue pools of his eyes, almost piercing in their intensity, seemed to swallow her, a striking contrast to his dark hair and swarthy skin. It wasn't as if she'd never seen a good-looking man before, but his European and Amerindian features blended together to create a perfect storm of masculine beauty.

"Didn't anyone ever tell you it's not polite to stare?" she asked.

"Can you blame me? You put on quite a show, Samirah."

Sah-meerr-ah.

Having traveled all over the world, and with Miami as her home base, she was quite familiar with accents. Still, the sound of his voice, with his rich Spanish intonation saying her name, caused goose bumps to prickle her skin.

Samirah shrugged. "I like to have fun."

"Have you ever won?"

"If I win tonight"—she held up three fingers—"it'll be three weeks running."

"After such enthusiastic applause, I can't imagine anyone else robbing you of the title."

"Neither can I."

Samirah knew her singing sucked, as did most people who

sang karaoke. To differentiate herself from the rest, she put on a big performance, and the audience loved it.

No one could really understand how much "I Will Survive" resonated with her after the rough six months she'd had back in Miami. After the embarrassment of getting fired from a job she loved, for months she hadn't been able to find employment, and the tiny balance in her bank account had dwindled to zero. Her refrigerator had been so empty, if she'd yelled into it she would have heard an echo.

Ecuador's currency was the U.S. dollar. If she managed to make as much tonight as she had the other nights, she would have over a thousand dollars to put in her savings. Not bad for five minutes a week.

"You're very confident."

Samirah laughed. "If I don't believe in myself, who will?"

"True." He picked up his bottle of beer and took a sip. "So where are you from, Samirah?"

"I like to think of myself as a citizen of the world."

"Are you always so evasive?"

She smirked. "Daddy taught me never to talk to strangers. Consider yourself lucky I've carried on a conversation with you for the last few minutes."

She took a good look at him, letting her eyes travel over his longish hair, swept back from his face to fall against the collar of his long-sleeved shirt. The white color emphasized the tan hue of his complexion. Her eyes settled below the open button where a necklace made of black cord rested against his chest. The cord supported a few colorful beads, in the middle of which hung the sharp white tooth of some predator.

His eyes narrowed to pale blue slits. "How can I get to know you better?"

"You can't. Don't get me wrong," she added hastily. "You're an attractive man, but I don't feel like being bothered."

One thick brow jumped in surprise. He probably wasn't used

to being turned down. She couldn't believe she'd managed to do it herself, considering how attractive she found him.

"So you think I'm a bother?"

"Like I said, don't take it the wrong way, but I'm not in Ecuador for long."

"All the more reason why we should get to know each other quickly."

She cocked a brow at him. "Do you ever give up?"

"Not when I see something I want," he drawled.

Samirah had fallen for enough bad boys to know when she met one. Underneath the unassuming white shirt and jeans and the clean-shaven face lurked danger. She was certain of it.

"I'm flattered, but I'll have to pass." She feigned disinterest, even though her pulse fluttered at the thought of getting to know him better. But with the drama she'd left behind in Miami, she'd made a promise to enjoy her short stay and treat it as an extended vacation. She would remain focused, which meant no men allowed.

"Pity," he murmured.

Samirah flipped her hair over one shoulder and cast a side-long glance in his direction. She wasn't opposed to having a fling. In fact, the number of men she'd slept with would have her pastor father dropping to his knees to pray for her soul. However, with less than two months left in her Ecuador assignment, and a vow she'd made to herself and her older sister, she didn't want to get involved with anyone at the moment—though he certainly threatened the durability of her resolve.

"It's a matter of using good common sense," she said, as if she lived by those rules every day.

"And there is nothing I can do to change your mind?"

"Nope."

"Even if I get Seth to vouch for me?"

He was nothing if not persistent. "It seems like your English is not so good. Let me spell it out for you so you can understand. N-O."

A young man, a regular who looked barely old enough to be in a bar, walked up. With an awkward glance at the Ecuadorian, he asked, "Samirah, you want to come sit with us?"

"Sure, John." She flashed the young man her best smile and picked up her glass. "Nice to meet you," she said to the stranger.

With a wave of her fingers, she followed behind the younger man. After a few steps, she turned to find the hunk at the bar now on his feet, watching her intently with a half-smile on his face. He eyed her backside like he wanted to bend her over right then and there, and her breath stopped somewhere in her throat.

Their eyes locked, and a shiver passed down her spine. For the space of a few seconds, she toyed with the idea of giving in. He met her standard criteria: tall, unusually so for an Ecuadorian—about six-three—and male. What her sister didn't know... no, *no*. A promise was a promise. Her impulsive nature had gotten her into several jams over the years, and this time she would err on the side of safe and boring.

With an exaggerated sway of her hips, Samirah headed over to one of the tables to sit with the group of young men and wait for the results of the karaoke competition.

CHAPTER 2

$\mathcal{T}$he bus squealed to a stop, and Samirah reached for the bag at her feet. The colorful silk scarf on her head corralled her thick hair and kept the strands from falling into her face as she bent to pick up the tote. After she slung it over her shoulder, she stepped down off the bus to walk the few blocks to the house.

Her trip into town had netted some good deals. The tote contained enough fruits and vegetables to last for the next few days, and peeking out the top of the bag was a colorful arrangement of fresh flowers purchased at the flower market.

One and two-story homes lined the neighborhood street she traveled down, painted in a palette of bright colors like rose, turquoise, and mustard yellow. In the mixed neighborhood, foreign transplants lived among natives, and bachelors mingled with families. *Cumbia* music, a popular Colombian import, poured from the open window of one of the houses.

"*Buenas tardes, Senorita* Samirah!"

She waved and smiled at the young boys playing soccer in the street. She waved again at the old matron sitting in the second floor window, keeping an eye on the goings on in the neighborhood. Nearby, a group of girls jumped rope and sang a song in Spanish. Normally, Samirah would stop and jump with them for a few minutes, but her time was short today because she'd idled over lunch and browsed some of the shops looking for souvenirs to send to her family. She always mailed the souvenirs so she wouldn't have the hassle of carrying extra baggage on the return trip home.

She couldn't believe three weeks had passed since she arrived. For the past ten years, she'd traveled all over the world, but Cuenca was turning out to be one of her favorite places by far. UNESCO had declared Cuenca's historic center a World Heritage Site, and rightly so. The charming city's cobblestone streets held an old-world charm with their plazas and ancient churches. Colonial-era buildings housed hotels, restaurants, and shops.

She also felt at home here. The food was exceptional with fresh ingredients readily available at the local markets. Getting around in Ecuador's third largest city was as simple as catching the bus or walking, so most expats didn't even own cars. The friendly, easy-going people made her stay enjoyable, including the British couple who had hired her, Geneva and Thomas Hill. They treated her more like family than a live-in housekeeper.

Samirah cringed inwardly.

She hated the word "housekeeper," but in truth, they didn't need only a personal chef. They didn't care if she had a certificate in the culinary arts from Le Cordon Bleu. They also didn't care she'd been traveling the world mastering her craft in various establishments and homes of the wealthy across the globe since the age of nineteen. They were paying an obscene amount of money—money she could put to good use in the pursuit of her dream of opening her own restaurant—so she wasn't complaining.

"Good afternoon, Samirah." The slowly-spoken greeting

came from a middle-aged man walking his dog. He liked to practice his English whenever he saw her.

She spoke slowly, too, to make it easier for him to understand. "Hello. How are you today?"

"I am fine. And you?"

"I'm doing well. Where are you going?" Samirah patted the dog's head.

"I am bringing the dog for a walk. Later, I will bringing the dog back home and then I am going to the store." He looked pleased with himself for tackling such a long sentence.

"Good," Samirah said. "But remember, it's I am *taking* the dog for a walk, and I will *bring* the dog back home."

"*Ay*! I forget again." He shook his head in disgust.

"It's okay." She winked at him and patted his shoulder. "You're getting better."

"*Gracias*." With a shy smile, he moved on.

Samirah opened the wrought iron gate and walked through the yard to let herself into the house. At the threshold, she removed her sandals and entered the modern kitchen, which flowed into an open great room. When she'd first seen the kitchen, she'd practically drooled over the Professional Series stainless steel Viking appliances. They were a testament to Geneva's love of cooking, something the older woman would temporarily have to forego until the hip therapy enabled her to move around like she used to.

She set her bag on the granite countertop and placed the flowers in a vase on the accent table in front of the window with a view of the street. After putting away most of the food, she spread out the items she planned to use for dinner.

Meal preparation was always her favorite part of the day. Tonight she would fix a traditional Ecuadorian dish, *encebollado de pescado*. The tasty fish soup filled with tuna, pickled onions, tomatoes, and yucca was not only hearty, but considered to be a good cure for a hangover.

Samirah smiled to herself. No hangovers here. The Hills didn't drink, and with her low tolerance for alcohol, she seldom did either. Humming to herself, she reached for a tomato, but she paused as a thought came into her head.

A glance at the clock told her she had time for a quick dip in the pool. She loved to swim. *Forty-five minutes, tops,* she promised herself. She would have to be out of the pool and have dinner ready by the time the Hills arrived, but she could do it.

After only a few seconds more hesitation, Samirah placed the soup ingredients in the fridge and went into her private quarters on the first floor. The three-room suite consisted of a bathroom, a combined living room and kitchen, and her bedroom. The living room contained a sofa, recliner, and a couple of accent tables. A two-burner stove and small refrigerator made up the kitchen. The best part of the bedroom was the French doors that led out onto a small patio in the backyard. She changed into a white halter-top string bikini and grabbed a towel.

Shortly after her arrival, she'd discovered a loose fence board while watering the plants. She made her way across the yard to it now. With the panel pushed aside, she turned sideways and slipped into the yard next door. The owner was out of the country and a pool cleaning service came in twice per week to clean and make sure the chemicals remained at an acceptable level.

Samirah dropped her towel over the back of one of the patio chairs and gracefully dived into the pool with a small splash, resurfacing a few feet away.

* * *

IN HIS DOWNSTAIRS STUDIO, Miguel heard what sounded like a splash in the pool. He sighed. Very few people knew he was back, and he guessed it was one of the neighborhood kids who didn't realize he was now at home. While out of the country, he'd kept the gate locked, giving only the pool service company a key. The last thing he'd wanted was to have one of the kids in the neighborhood using his pool unattended because of the risk of drowning.

He pushed the wheeled stool back from his latest creation, a four-foot image of an indigenous woman bent over a basket of fruit. The three-dimensional woman protruded from a rectangular block of plaster fitted around her like a frame.

He was luckier than most. His work continued to sell well despite the fact that he hadn't done a tour in years. He already had a New York buyer for this one, sight unseen. Once completed, his agent would arrange to have it picked up and shipped.

Miguel stood with the mallet and chisel he'd been using to carve her feet and walked across the dusty, plaster-covered floor. At the window, the afternoon sun warmed his bare chest. He looked out into the back yard and drew in a sharp breath at the unexpected image of a woman with chocolate-colored skin easing her way across the pool with her long hair dragging on the surface behind her. Within seconds, he recognized her.

Well, well. What have we here?

She swam several laps, using an unhurried pace as her arms sliced through the water before turning over to float on her back.

The poorly lit bar had not done her justice. Her body was full and ripe in all the right places, and the skimpy bikini enhanced every dip and curve. As his eyes roamed her body, the sting of attraction assailed him, tightening his gut and reminding him it had been months since he'd last touched a woman.

If he believed in destiny, he would think she had been served up on a platter by fate, his for the taking. But that's not how real life worked, and he knew that all too well. The only question to be answered now was, how had she ended up in his pool?

* * *

WITH HER EYES CLOSED, Samirah relaxed after swimming several laps, enjoying the feeling of weightlessness in the water.

Another beautiful day, she mused to herself.

Too bad she would have to give up her secret indulgence when the owner came back. She hoped he would stay gone for at least a couple more weeks, but with her luck, he'd probably show up tomorrow. According to Geneva, he was a sculptor. She hoped he was the neighborly type. If so, maybe she could convince him to allow her to use the pool from time to time.

All of a sudden, Samirah had the eerie feeling she was being watched. A frown marred her forehead as she drifted along in the water with her arms outstretched. Her eyes flew open, unease settling in her stomach. She let her gaze travel to the fence. She shifted it to the right, the left, and back to the front again.

Nothing.

Her lids lowered and she smiled to herself. Guilt could do that to a person. People who engaged in behavior they shouldn't often had the feeling they were being watched, and she had no business in the neighbor's pool.

Moving her arms like oars, she created little ripples and glided slowly through the water.

The prickly sensation persisted. She ignored it at first, but soon it became unbearable and her heartbeat accelerated. She opened her eyes again, looking around. Although she could see into this yard from upstairs in the house where she stayed, the Hills weren't home yet, so that didn't explain the uneasiness. Fruit trees blocked the view of the pool from the house on the other side. Still, the odd feeling remained.

Then she heard something—movement—behind her. She didn't imagine it. She froze, listening. Even though the sound didn't repeat, she knew whatever or whoever was there hadn't left.

Tilting her head back in the water at an awkward angle to see behind her, Samirah saw the culprit. It wasn't a stray cat as she'd secretly hoped.

It was a man. The hunk from the bar!

He'd disappeared not long after she'd walked away from him last night. Now he stood staring down at her with his hands on his hips.

Her eyes widened and every muscle in her body tensed, which caused her to sink below the surface of the water. She splashed wildly for a moment before kicking her feet to right herself. Treading water in the deep end, she stared up at him in shock.

He hadn't moved.

"Having fun?" he asked in a dry tone.

Her mind blanked, distracted by the hard muscles of his chest and washboard abs. He'd been hiding quite a body beneath the shirt she saw him in last night, a classic male shape of broad shoulders and lean hips covered by a pair of khaki-colored linen slacks that hung low on his narrow waist. A half-inch of pelvic bone jutted above the waistband and captured her attention. Clearly the drawstrings were not as tight as they should be to keep the pants properly secured.

"Did you follow me?" she demanded when she found the wherewithal to look away.

He seemed taken aback. "I was about to ask you the same question."

His voice poured over her like warm syrup. She swallowed, one part of her registering the undeniable tug of attraction to this golden-skinned god, the other part not sure if she should panic or not.

"This is private property, and you're trespassing. What are you doing here?" No sooner had the words left her lips, Samirah got a sinking feeling in the pit of her stomach. He appeared way too relaxed and was half-dressed. She suspected she wouldn't like the answer.

"I live here," he replied. Her stomach plummeted. "What are *you* doing here?"

Oh boy.

CHAPTER 3

$\mathcal{N}$ ine times out of ten, whenever Samirah found herself in a sticky situation, it was because she'd said or done something she shouldn't have. Only one time out of ten could she honestly say she found herself in a situation not of her own doing. This was not one of those times.

"You're the owner, the artist."

It was a statement of dread rather than a question, and she knew she'd have a lot of explaining to do. This was the famed sculptor Geneva had gushed about—Delgado, Ecuador's pride and joy. Now she understood the reason for his incredible physique. As an artist who sculpted using plaster, he would have to lift heavy bags on a regular basis and reposition his sculptures from time to time. To think she'd met him last night and didn't have a clue to his identity.

"Correct. Miguel Delgado."

"You're supposed to be in Miami."

"I'm sorry to disappoint you, but I came back yesterday." His steady gaze didn't waver. "You mentioned something about trespassing?"

Samirah opened her mouth to speak and promptly closed it.

She experienced a rare occasion where she couldn't think of a single adequate answer. She was busted.

Miguel leaned forward and extended a hand to her. Reluctantly, she took it and allowed him to lever her out of the pool.

Once she stood before him, he didn't let her go right away. He held onto her arm and looked down at her from a good nine inches, his face unreadable. His heated gaze made her feel as if he'd brushed his hand down the front of her body and made her very aware of the fact that the bathing suit, although in good condition, fit tight because she'd gained weight since purchasing it years ago. Her fuller breasts were squeezed tightly together and pushed above the edge of the top.

She became conscious of the part of her anatomy where his eyes lingered. A tank of oxygen would do her well right now, and a pair of industrial-thick oven mitts that came all the way up to her elbow to prevent the skin of her forearm from scorching in his grasp.

Under normal circumstances, Samirah prided herself on being in control, but right now, she felt decidedly weak and—unsafe. The promises she'd made to herself before taking this trip suddenly seemed under threat of ruin.

"May I have my towel, please?" she said softly, not trusting her legs to support her walking around him to retrieve it where she'd tossed it over the chair.

He seemed reluctant to release her. When he did, he prolonged it, letting his slightly rough fingers drag along the sensitive skin of the inside of her arm. His warm touch sent tingles to settle in her breasts, making the nipples harden in an embarrassing way. Once freed, her arm hung limply at her side. He turned around to get the towel, giving her a good view of his muscular back, which tapered up into an impressive vee from the waistband of his pants.

She pressed her lips together and pulled them inward to fight back a whimper as she imagined smoothing her hands across the sinewy muscles. There wasn't an ounce of fat on his bronze body. Could she have picked a worse time to try to be good?

He handed her the towel, and Samirah donned it like a cloak of protection, her only defense against the invasion of warm sensations evoked by his nearness. She wrapped the towel tightly around her body like a giant bandage and tucked it securely under one arm.

Feeling stronger, she laughed guiltily. "This isn't what it looks like."

The scarred brow rose. "Oh really? You mean you weren't swimming in my pool without my permission? Because that's what it looks like. Have you been sleeping in my bed and eating my porridge, too?"

Her face heated at the Goldilocks reference, which under normal circumstances would be comical since physically she was probably as far removed from Goldilocks as a person could get. Unfortunately, she didn't know how to read Miguel yet and needed to get on his good side. So far he didn't appear upset, but she'd rebuffed him last night and he might still be nursing a bruised ego.

"Not exactly. I—"

"And please, speak slowly so I can understand. It seems my English is not so good." He folded his arms across his muscled chest. He wasn't cutting her any slack, using her own words from last night against her.

Taking a deep breath, Samirah launched into an explanation. "Obviously I've been using your pool while you were gone, but not very often."

"How often is 'not very often?'" His disapproving face reminded her of the many times she'd been called into the principal's office as a teenager for one infraction or another.

She shrugged like it was no big deal. "Only on Tuesdays and Thursdays." They happened to be the same two days Thomas took Geneva to the hospital for physical therapy. With them out of the house, no one would see her in the pool. "We're neighbors, you know," she said, trying to appeal to his sense of community. She tilted her head toward the house.

Miguel frowned. "The Hills live over there."

"Yes, and I've been staying with them the past few weeks. I'm the new housekeeper."

"New housekeeper?" he repeated in disbelief, quickly running his eyes over her. "You do not look like a housekeeper."

"Well, I am. Monday through Friday I cook the meals, do light housekeeping, and run errands. The maid they've had for the past few years continues to come in on the weekend to do the heavy cleaning and laundry."

"That doesn't explain how you ended up in my pool."

She suspected no explanation she gave would be satisfactory. So much for staying out of trouble on this trip. "I know what I did was wrong, but I swear I only intended to do it one time. Except, I enjoyed myself so much, I continued to come." She could very well be digging a deeper hole for herself. When he didn't respond, the silence unnerved her. "I know that's no excuse, but it's the truth. Are you going to tell my employers?"

She couldn't afford to be fired from another job. Even though the Hills liked her and appreciated her work, she didn't know how they would respond to sneaking onto the neighbor's property.

"Should I?"

"I don't see why. It could be our little secret."

Miguel ran his knuckles along the underside of his chin. "As you pointed out a few minutes ago, you were trespassing. I don't know if I should let such bad behavior go unpunished."

The fact that he didn't want her behavior to go unpunished didn't cause quite the concern it should. Maybe because when he looked at her from beneath lowered lids, he didn't look as if the punishment he had in mind would result in any physical discomfort on her part.

Samirah swallowed. "I know I didn't endear myself to you last night, and now this—but I'm a nice person. And was any harm done?" Once again, he wouldn't respond, and she felt the need to break the silence. "No harm done, right?"

He seemed to think about it for a moment. "No harm done," he agreed.

"So...we're good?" She held her breath, ready for whatever would come.

"Don't worry, I won't say anything to the Hills."

She almost collapsed from relief. "Thank you."

He looked down at her thoughtfully. "I understand Geneva is a very good cook, so you must be very good as well to satisfy her requirements."

Samirah lifted her chin. "I'm excellent. I received my training from Le Cordon Bleu." His eyebrows flew upward at the mention of the prestigious culinary school. "I've been traveling the world since I was nineteen, building on the basics I learned there. At my last job, I was the head cook."

She may mess up other areas of her life, but few could match her skills in the kitchen. She'd inherited her passion for cooking from her Caribbean-born mother, who was known to prepare meals large enough to feed a small army.

"If you have so much experience, why then are you a housekeeper?"

The question surprised her, and she glanced away to avoid his eyes. "I'm in between jobs."

She told the truth, but there was way more to it. Of course she would much rather be in a restaurant cooking or preparing professional meals for wealthy clients, enabling her to use the training and skills she'd acquired over the years. In fact, her position as head cook had been at a large hotel restaurant in Miami until she lost her job.

How could she explain she'd been forced out, practically wearing a scarlet "A" emblazoned on her chest? She'd made a big mistake when she slept with her boss, the executive chef at the restaurant in the five star hotel where she had worked. She had thought she was in love with him, and he with her. Her foolish romantic thoughts cost her a job she loved. Next year she would be thirty, and the position had been a way for her to start setting down roots and leave her nomadic lifestyle behind. Too late, she'd found out he was married—an important piece of information he'd failed to share with her.

Before the confrontation with his wife, the wagging tongues of her co-workers in the restaurant and other hotel staff had made her feel like an outcast. It wasn't long before the owners made a decision. The choice was simple. There was no contest between a cook and an executive chef. She left her job, humiliated but wiser.

"I apologize if I offended you," Miguel said.

"You didn't." Samirah squared her shoulders and shook off the feelings of regret that stole into her consciousness. There was no point in beating herself up over what happened. "Like I said, I'm an excellent cook, and the Hills are happy."

"Are you familiar with Ecuadorian cuisine?"

Samirah nodded, eyeing him suspiciously.

This time, he chuckled, and the sound generated warmth in the depths of her belly. "You look as if you don't trust me. Shouldn't I be the one concerned, since you sneaked onto my property without permission?"

"I'm not concerned, I'm just wondering where you're going with your line of questioning."

"Nowhere, except I thought maybe one day you could have pity on a poor, helpless bachelor and fix me a meal some time." He looked anything but helpless. With his rugged good looks, she suspected he had a legion of women clamoring to cook his meals—among other things.

"Maybe," she said slowly.

"One meal, one day when you're free. That's not too much to ask for not speaking to the Hills, is it?"

"No, I guess not." Then she added, "Saturdays are best, because it's my day off, and I could—"

"I'll let you know when I want you."

His words jolted her, causing a rush of heat to suffuse her breasts. The way they slid off his tongue, deliberate and slow, made her feel what he said and what he meant were very different. It could be a nuance of language, or it could be he knew exactly what he was saying and was making good use of double entendres.

"All right." She took a quivering breath. "Since we're in agreement, I'll be on my way."

"How about we shake on it?" He extended his hand.

Samirah hesitated. Silly, really, because it was only a hand, but she felt a nervous tremor inside. She looked down at his long, tan fingers as if they were a rattlesnake getting ready to strike.

"I won't bite." Almost immediately, her mind extended his words to, *Unless you want me to.*

She placed her hand in his, and he enclosed hers in a warm clasp. There was nothing remotely sexual about a handshake, but she felt his touch to her very core, and when she looked up at him, the heat in his blue eyes made the breath lodge in her throat.

"Thank you, Mr. Delgado." She tried to pull away, but his grip tightened.

"Call me Miguel. There's no need for such formality between neighbors." A smile touched his sensuous lips.

"Thank you, Miguel." She tugged harder this time, and he released her.

Without another word, Samirah left the way she came, practically fleeing across the yard. She maintained her stride, even though her legs developed a disturbing rubbery texture that made it difficult to walk. She felt his eyes on her the entire time.

* * *

MIGUEL WATCHED her walk away and slip back between the boards of the fence. He wanted her. Badly. Holding onto her soft hand, he could hardly think of anything else but dragging her closer and crushing her mouth under his. Was she that soft all over? Did her wild streak translate into the bedroom?

He was no fool. Despite her refusal to engage him at the bar, he recognized the interest in her eyes. The extra swing she'd added to her hips last night to tease him when she walked away had only served to confirm it.

He shook his head in an effort to dispel the image of Samirah's dark, wet skin in the revealing suit, but it didn't work. The triangular material of the bikini left little to the imagination, not doing a very good job of covering her generous breasts, which overflowed over the top and sides of the barely there material. The thin straps appeared ready to snap, unable to contain their immense package.

He stared into the pool, remembering her fluid movements in the water. A woman like her would be perfect. They could have a brief affair that ended when she left. No demands for a relationship and no unwanted publicity.

Miguel made his way back into the house. It might be fun to get to know her better. Maybe it was his lucky day. Maybe fate had served her up on a platter for him after all.

CHAPTER 4

*S*amirah took a quick shower, shampooed her hair, and blow dried it straight. She pulled her hair back and slipped on a tank top and a comfortable pair of jeans before returning to the kitchen.

From the window, she could see Miguel's house, and her heart still raced after seeing him again. Although she realized he could have complained about her, somehow she'd managed to dodge that bullet.

Her brother Adam had gotten her this job, sourcing it through his international placement firm. It had been a lifeline because she'd become upset over the difficulty she'd experienced finding another steady job after she was let go from the hotel. She couldn't risk giving her brother's company a bad reputation. He would never forgive her if she did. Hell, she would never forgive herself.

Samirah returned to the task of cooking dinner and had the pot simmering on the stove when a taxi pulled up outside the gate and her employers descended. Geneva's limited mobility had prompted them to hire outside help. Cost had been no object, as Thomas was a retired executive from a top investment firm. The Hills had been living in Cuenca for almost five years, lured by the low crime rate, comfortable year-round climate, and the low cost of living.

They were two very active seniors, and the limitations brought about by the accident curtailed their activities. They had photos on the walls and in albums showcasing their pastimes, including horseback riding, sports fishing, and cycling.

Samirah watched Geneva use her walker and move gingerly up the walkway. As they rounded the corner of the house, she went to the front door and flung it wide.

"Hey, there, how was it today?" she asked in a cheery voice. She'd learned right away Geneva did not like her therapy sessions, and she could be grumpy for hours afterward if she and Thomas didn't find a way to lift her spirits.

"Horrible. Simply horrible," the other woman grumbled. She set her walker at the bottom of the three steps she had to climb. "Thomas, stop hovering," she snapped over her shoulder.

Seeing the man's exasperated expression, Samirah gave him a sympathetic smile and wink over his wife's head.

"Come on, Geneva, you know he's only trying to help." She retrieved the walker and set it inside the door.

"I can do it myself," Geneva said.

She placed her hands on the black handrails Thomas installed after her surgery. Geneva had missed her footing on these steps and broken her hip when she fell. Samirah had heard Thomas say on several occasions if he'd had the railings installed in the first place, the accident wouldn't have happened. Even though Geneva didn't blame him, he was still filled with guilt.

Thomas continued to hover behind his wife as she grasped tightly onto the black metal with both hands and hoisted herself up one stair. "There you go," he coaxed.

"*Thomas*," Geneva warned.

Samirah stood back and watched the older woman, on alert to stabilize her in case she couldn't make it. She had already made progress in the short time Samirah had been living with them. When she first moved in, it had taken both her and Thomas to help Geneva up the stairs. She could do it on her own now, but it was a slow, harrowing process.

Minutes later, Geneva stood on the threshold, breathing heavily from the effort. Tiny beads of perspiration had popped out on her upper lip. Her short, silver hair was damp around her forehead.

"Just a few more steps," the older woman said to herself. She rested her hands on the walker and started the journey to the great room.

"Looking good," Thomas added, to his wife's exasperation.

Finally, Geneva breathed a heavy sigh and settled onto the sofa with a pillow at her back. Two large ceiling fans circulated cooling air throughout the room. "Smells good in here."

"The soup will soon be finished." Samirah took ice water to each of them. "What did the therapist say about your progress?"

"She said I'm coming along well and maintains six to seven more weeks of therapy should suffice. I can hardly wait. The pain is unbearable, and I absolutely hate the therapy sessions."

Thomas mumbled something. "What was that?" Geneva asked sharply.

"Nothing, my love."

The corners of Samirah's lips lifted upward. "I'm glad to hear your recovery is going well."

"Yes, it's unfortunate what happened. As we get older, we become clumsier, and the old bones are not what they used to be." Geneva sighed heavily. "Oh, after you left this morning, we saw our neighbor, the artist. He's back from his trip to Miami."

No kidding. "How well do you know him?"

"Not well, my dear. He's not the friendliest chap, but we've spoken a few times. He seldom has company, and I don't think

I've ever seen him have a woman over there, unless he scuttles them in at night. His mother's the only woman I've seen him with, and that was about two years ago when she and his little brother came for a visit, wasn't it, Thomas?"

Thomas nodded his agreement.

"I met him last night at the bar where I go to sing karaoke, but I didn't know he was the artist you referred to as Delgado." Samirah's contract required her to be available to the Hills at night should they need her, but they did allow her the indulgence of going to karaoke once per week for a couple of hours.

She went to the kitchen to finish the dinner preparation.

"At karaoke?" Geneva asked in an incredulous voice.

Samirah smiled at the woman's tone. "He said he and Seth are friends."

"Oh, that makes more sense. I couldn't imagine him participating in Karaoke Night."

Thomas chuckled. "Certainly not. He doesn't strike me as the type."

"True. He tends to keep to himself—a very low key young fellow. His sculptures are wonderful, though. The large ones are my favorites, Samirah. They're huge and depict the life of the indigenous people of Ecuador. Beautiful. Absolutely beautiful."

Samirah retrieved dinner rolls from the oven and set them on a cooling rack on the counter. "How much do his pieces sell for?" she asked, as she brushed melted butter and honey across the tops of the hot bread.

"It's obscene. Absolutely obscene," Geneva said, though Samirah could hear the adoration in her voice. "I heard he sold one of his pieces to a private European collector last year for almost a hundred thousand dollars."

Samirah's movements stilled. "No way."

"It's true," Thomas confirmed. "The deal was struck in Miami, and apparently a bidding war broke out between the two collectors, which inflated the price. The European collector won, and he had his personal curator fly into Miami to complete the purchase and accompany the sculpture back to... Spain, I think."

"I'm in the wrong business. I shouldn't be cooking, I should be sculpting!"

"You and me both!"

The three of them laughed.

From the corner of her eye, Samirah saw Geneva nudge Thomas.

After clearing his throat, Thomas said, "Samirah, my dear, I have an awfully big favor to ask of you."

"Thomas, if you begin like that, she's bound to say no."

He sighed. "We told you about the fundraiser at the University of Cuenca to benefit the arts. Well, we had purchased two tickets before Geneva's accident. It's little more than a week away, and she won't be up to attending, of course." Regret filled his voice.

"But he can go," his wife added.

"I'd rather not go without you and leave you here alone." Samirah smiled at the sweetness behind Thomas's words.

"I'll be fine." Geneva took over the conversation. "Samirah, my dear, we thought you might like to go to the event with Thomas—keep him company, and then we won't waste the other ticket. You can keep an eye on him for me to keep the floozies away."

Samirah choked back a giggle. She couldn't recall the last time she'd heard the word floozy—if ever. "I would love to go." She halted her preparations. "I'm guessing it's a formal event?"

"Black tie is required, so you'll need a nice cocktail dress or a gown."

"Shouldn't be a problem. I could go to the mall and shop for an outfit."

She was almost four hundred dollars richer after her karaoke win, which meant she could afford to splurge on herself. The last time she'd been to an event that required she get dressed up was when her sister and husband renewed their vows four years ago. It might be fun to get dressed up and mingle with a different crowd.

"Splendid!" Geneva said. "But since we're asking such a big favor of you, take time off tomorrow to go shopping." She beamed happily. "You'll have such a lovely time, Samirah. We've gone the past few years, and I must say I'm always impressed by all the lovely art the students produce. They donate original pieces, and at the end, they're auctioned to raise money. The auction has grown quite a bit, and this is the first time it's taking place at the university. Someone knew someone who knows the chair of the art department, and he agreed to allow the event to take place there."

"Sounds like fun, and I don't mind going, but what about you, Geneva? Will you be all right here alone? In your condition?"

"I have to agree with her, my dear," Thomas piped up. She could well understand the concern etched in Thomas's face.

"Poppycock! I'll be just fine, and Samirah, I'm sure you'll find something suitable at the local mall. Thomas, you will go and have a good time. I won't hear another word about it."

"My dear—"

Geneva shook her head stubbornly. "Go, have a good time, and bring back something we can hang on the wall."

"Well...if you think you'll be all right..." He looked doubtful.

"If you're sure," Samirah began, "I'm fine with it. I'll keep the floozies away from him."

"It's settled," Geneva said in a resolute voice.

After dinner, Thomas began the arduous task of helping his wife up the stairs to their bedroom since she refused to set up a bed downstairs. Samirah knew they wouldn't be back down for the rest of the evening, but if they needed her, they could call the private line in her suite. She washed the dishes and straightened up the living room before going to bed.

Her mind strayed to Miguel next door. She'd managed to keep thoughts of him at bay during most of the night, but now those thoughts encroached, and with them the reminder of his touch and the way his long fingers had stroked along the inside of her arm.

Lucky for her she didn't have any reason to interact with him again. If Geneva was correct about him keeping mostly to himself, it would be easy to steer clear of him. She probably didn't even have to concern herself with cooking a meal for him. All she had to worry about right now was finding a dress for the fundraiser.

Miguel Delgado was the least of her worries.

CHAPTER 5

On Wednesday, Samirah ran some personal errands in town before catching the bus to the mall late in the afternoon. She hated shopping, though, and finding a dress she liked might be difficult. She tended to be picky, preferring to wear clothing she felt expressed her individuality and personality.

Dressed comfortably in a pair of tennis shoes, shorts, and a T-shirt with a rhinestone design on the front, she visited several stores before wandering into a boutique. She explained the type of outfit she needed and the occasion. The salesperson, who turned out to be the owner, showed her several black dresses, but Samirah didn't like any of them.

"I'm not going to a funeral," she said to the woman in Spanish. "Do you have anything with brighter colors? Maybe red or blue, or even green?"

The woman pursed her lips and looked Samirah up and down. "I have a few you might like."

She took her over to a rack and one by one withdrew dresses in different styles, holding up each one to get Samirah's approval. Before long, they'd chosen three and Samirah went into the small dressing room to try on the first one. A few minutes later, she emerged and stood holding up the bodice of the too-large strapless dress. It would have to be altered, but she liked the way the fabric felt against her skin and the ankle-length hem made her feel elegant.

"What do you think?"

"Absolutely beautiful," a male voice said. She whirled around to see Miguel against the wall. The sight of him made her heart slam against her chest so sharply she didn't doubt the next day her ribs would be bruised. He looked like he was holding up the wall with one shoulder, in a pair of faded jeans covering his long legs, casually crossed at the ankles. "It looks too big for you, though."

"Are you following me *now*?" Samirah asked.

With an indolent smile, he straightened and came toward her. His clear blue eyes held a bit of mischief, and she realized she would be in trouble before he opened his mouth. "I was passing by when I saw you go into the dressing room to change. I thought I might be able to offer some assistance."

"How kind of you," Samirah said, her voice edged with sarcasm, "but I don't need any assistance."

"It would be helpful to get a male point of view, don't you think?" He asked the question in Spanish and looked at the shop owner for concurrence, which she readily offered.

"Another opinion is always helpful," the woman said, watching them with interest.

Helpful for whom? Samirah wanted to know. Miguel said something to the woman in Quichua, the second most popular language spoken in Ecuador. It dated back to the time of the Incas, and Samirah didn't speak a word of it. The woman laughed and responded to him.

"What did you say to her?" Samirah demanded.

"Nothing important."

"It is important, or you would have said it in Spanish so I could understand. It's very rude of you to speak in another language so I can't understand."

He spoke again to the boutique owner, and she giggled. She said a few words back to him, bestowing a smile on both of them, similar to that of a doting grandmother.

Samirah swung back to him and rolled her eyes. "Okay, what did you say *that* time?"

"Well, if you must know..."

"Yes, I must."

"I told her we had a lovers' quarrel, and you're angry with me, but I can help you pick your dress from here."

Samirah swung back to the woman, making sure to clutch the slipping gown to her chest to maintain coverage over her breasts. *"No es verdad. Él es un mentiroso."*

He didn't seem to mind that she called him a liar. He gave a self-deprecating shrug, as if to prove his point to the owner, and then spoke again in Quichua. The two of them carried on a conversation, none of which Samirah comprehended. She tapped her foot, waiting for them to finish. At the end of it, the boutique owner walked away.

"Where is she going?"

"She's giving us some privacy. She's a kind woman—a romantic."

"Did she understand you were lying to her when you told her we're lovers?"

"For some reason, she didn't believe your accusation that I wasn't telling the truth. I wonder why."

"Because whatever you said to her carried more weight than what I said."

"I am her countryman after all." He moved closer, and Samirah pressed her heels into the carpet to keep from backing up.

"Maybe this kind of behavior works on the women here, but it won't on me." At least she hoped not. Even though she maintained a look of steel, her resolve was dissolving faster than a cube of ice on hot coals.

"You'd be surprised." She wouldn't, actually. "Now, let's take a look at the dress." He made a circular motion in the air with his forefinger, indicating she should do a twirl.

"If you think," Samirah said through thinned lips, "I'm going to prance around so you can ogle me, think again. I'm going somewhere else to shop." She lifted her nose in the air and moved past him.

"Don't tell me this poor woman lost a sale because of me."

Samirah glanced at him over her shoulder. "You should've thought about that before you said what you did. I'm not modeling for you."

"Humor me."

"No."

"Don't punish her because of my behavior. At least try on the other dresses."

Conflicted, Samirah glared at him. On the one hand, she hated shopping and didn't want to have to deal with Miguel here to watch what she wore. On the other hand, if she didn't pick an outfit today, she'd be stuck having to come back out to the mall, and she really did want to try on the other dresses. One of them might be the one. If she left and came back another time, they might be gone, and she'd have to start all over again.

"If I do this, and I come out and show them to you, do you promise to behave?"

"As much as I can. I mean, yes."

With one final glare at him, Samirah turned away from his charming smile and hurried into the dressing room. "Nothing's going to happen," she mumbled to herself, slipping off the gown and putting on the other. "It's not like we're going to have sex right this minute."

The thought of wrapping her body around his left her breathless and weakened her knees. She reached toward the floor length mirror to stabilize herself. "Oh my goodness," she whispered. "Celibacy sucks."

Seconds later, wearing a halter-topped dress that also landed around her ankles, she emerged to find Miguel in the middle of the sales floor. Thrusting her shoulders back, she walked forward on bare feet, having left her tennis shoes behind.

Her hands went to her hips. "What do you think about this one?" She kept her voice arctic cold, sending him a message and hoping he couldn't see past her façade of phony cool indifference.

"Hmm." He tilted this head to the side, considering the dress. "Let me see." He walked around her, making her feel exceedingly uncomfortable, warming her body in secret places. "Hmm," he said again when he stood directly behind her. "I like the fit back here."

She was going to kill him. One one-thousand, two one-thousand . . .

He came back into view. "I like it better than the first one, but let's see the last one to make sure."

Samirah marched back into the dressing room and donned the other dress, reminding herself it would soon be over. This one was just as elegant, with a ruche bodice and a one-shoulder design. It gathered at the waist to show off her hourglass figure and the poly-jersey fabric stretched across her hips and buttocks before draping loosely around her legs thanks to a mid-thigh slit on the left side. The tomato color popped against her dark skin and as she critiqued her reflection, she realized this was her favorite of the three.

Because it was too long at the hem, she had to gather a couple of inches in her hand to keep from tripping before stepping out from behind the curtain. When she appeared before Miguel again, she right away saw the male appreciation in his eyes. The lazy grin he'd been sporting when she reappeared dissolved into a long, heat-filled look.

Walking on feet that barely managed to move her forward, she asked, "What do you think?"

Without a word, he circled her like a predatory wolf, and she remained as still as prey, thinking if she didn't move he wouldn't pounce. "This is the one."

"I agree," she said softly, unable to tear her eyes away from his steady stare.

The formerly comfortable dress felt tighter under the weight of his gaze. He was no longer the easy-going artist. A shiver down her spine warned her again of the danger. But it wasn't bodily harm—it was the ruination of her heart, possibly her soul, even, if she allowed him to get too close.

But she was already too close, joining in the game he had started. She was getting sucked into the vortex of her desire for him, and the pounding alert of her heart echoed in her skull, warning her that falling for a man like this would be far more devastating than the embarrassment she'd suffered at the restaurant in Miami.

She didn't know where she accessed the strength necessary to drag her eyes away, but she found it. "This is the one I'll get."

He didn't say a word, and she didn't look up at him for fear of what she would see. She walked away and once alone, she sagged against the wall.

SAMIRAH ARRANGED to have the dress picked up the next day after the hem had been taken up. To go with the dress, she purchased a pair of chandelier earrings and heels she would have to practice walking in before the big event. She avoided shoes with heels over two inches whenever she could, but a dress like this deserved a pair of sexy shoes to go with it.

"Can I buy you dinner?" Miguel asked once they'd stepped out of the store and she had her purchases in hand.

"No, thank you. I'm on my way back to the house."

"I could give you a lift. I'm headed back myself."

Samirah came to an abrupt stop, forcing the couple behind them to veer sharply to the left to avoid colliding into her. The man cursed angrily. She barely heard him because she was so focused on the six-foot-three Ecuadorian towering over her.

"No, thank you, I don't need a ride back," she said slowly, enunciating each word.

Miguel caught her chin between his thumb and forefinger. Warm, delicious sensations arrowed toward her abdomen. "How long do you plan to do this? How long do you plan to run from me?" he asked, looking down at her with hooded eyes.

"As long as it takes. You're wasting your time."

"I don't think so." His thumb stroked across the underside of her lower lip. She wanted to swat away his hand, but she couldn't, rendered helpless in the middle of a busy mall. "You strike me as a confident woman of adventure, so I have to ask— why? Did someone hurt you?"

The spell broke, and she freed herself, pulling back to clear her mind from the narcotic-like effect of his touch. "No."

He'd come so close to the truth of her shameful secret. The fact that a married man had used her as his plaything, and she'd never even known he was married. Her woman's intuition hadn't kicked in. When the rollercoaster ride of their whirlwind relationship had come to a crashing halt, she ended up losing her job and her reputation. No one believed she hadn't known he had a wife, but he'd managed to walk away practically unscathed, with his career and marriage intact.

Miguel peered at her with a frown, trying to decipher the complicated puzzle she presented. "Then why?"

"Did it ever occur to you that maybe I'm not interested?"

A muscle in his jaw pulsed. "No, it never occurred to me," he said. "Not when I can clearly see you want me as much as I want you. Not when I could have followed you into the dressing room moments ago and had you against the wall." He spoke the words with such raw intensity, her insides trembled. "No, Samirah, it never occurred to me."

She went still, unable to look at him, without the strength to deny the accuracy of his words. But she'd promised herself no sex on this trip. Besides, she barely knew him. The extent of her knowledge consisted of knowing he lived next door, and he sculpted. Nothing else.

"I can't sleep with you right now."

Why had she added those last two words, suggesting she would eventually, but not right this minute? Was it inevitable?

"Who said anything about sleeping?" The smile in his voice compelled her to raise her gaze to his. "Let me give you a ride home. That's all I'm offering."

She was being ridiculous. There was no harm in accepting a ride from him. Unless he attacked her in the car. "Okay," she said with a resigned note to her voice.

Out in the parking lot, Samirah realized they were walking toward a Harley Davidson motorcycle and pulled up short.

"Is that yours?"

"It is." He smiled at her. "You look surprised."

"Because I thought when you offered me a ride you meant you had a car." She drew nearer to the powerful-looking machine, admiring the shiny blue and chrome paint.

"I had it custom made and imported last year."

"It's nice, but I don't know if I would feel comfortable riding with you."

"I'm very careful. You have nothing to be afraid of."

Except being pressed up against you for the length of the ride back home. The short trip would seem like an eternity.

"You only have one helmet," she pointed out.

"And it's all yours." He released the lock and handed the helmet to her.

Miguel took her bag and deposited it in the leather saddlebag on the side and then swung one long leg over the machine. Over his shoulder, he asked, "Are you coming?"

Against her better judgment, Samirah pulled the helmet onto her head. In a moment of vanity, she wondered in dismay what her hair would look like once she removed the protective head gear.

Awkwardly, she swung her leg over the top of the machine and settled onto the seat.

"Hold onto me," Miguel instructed. "You'll need to lean when I lean, and turn when I turn to maintain balance on the bike. Got it?"

The tightening in her throat made it difficult to breathe. She'd been on a bike before, so that wasn't the problem. "Got it," she said with a shaky breath.

She wrapped her arms around him, her hard nipples poking into his muscular back. Miguel flipped the kill switch and pushed the start button, and they were on their way.

By the time they arrived at his house, Samirah was thankful women didn't get erections, or she would have a massive boner right now.

"Thank you for the ride," she whispered, retrieving her package. Keeping her eyes downcast, she moved away from him, trying to distance herself from the physical need of wanting him.

"Samirah." Her name left his lips on a groan.

She gasped when he grabbed her from behind and dragged her into the shadows, forcing her back against the wall of the house. Her package fell from her weakened grasp so she could grab onto the rigid muscles of his arms as he hauled her up and against his body. Weak-kneed and grateful for the supporting wall against her back, she gazed into his eyes. Air squeezed from her lungs as he locked their bodies together against the concrete and lifted her to press his loins between the cradle of her hips.

"Miguel...?"

His eyes blazed down at hers in the dimly lit yard. Then he lowered his head to forge a hungry kiss.

CHAPTER 6

*M*iguel had heard the shock in her voice, but he'd also heard the heated tremble, recognizing she felt the same untamed need that drove him. It consumed him —so much so he couldn't even make it to the door of his house.

The ride back had been both pleasurable and painful. He'd been tortured by the sensation of her breasts across his back and her fingers pressing into his abdomen. He'd planned to wear her down little by little over time, but that plan was tossed out. Right now he sported an erection hard enough to tunnel through granite and needed relief.

He didn't even try to stop himself. Why should he, when he'd wanted her since the moment he saw her on stage?

He plied her mouth with kisses, determined to dominate her senses the same way she had his, and pressed his throbbing erection even harder against her while his tongue filled her mouth. She tasted so much better than he ever imagined, making him tremble and ache. With the help of her legs clamped around his hips, he held her steady and pushed up her T-shirt to unhook the front clasp of her bra and release her bountiful breasts for his waiting mouth. They spilled from confinement like heavy fruit, and he groaned with pleasure.

Finally.

He kissed the dusky tips, her jagged breath arousing him just as much as her beautiful body. Then he captured one nipple, sucking it into a more rigid point, scraping his teeth across it until she shuddered and moaned.

"You're beautiful," he murmured as he pressed his face into the scented hollow between the soft mounds.

Her hands moved in a frenzy of motion across the back of his neck and stroked upward to cup his head as he showered kisses across her skin up to her throat. Panting and greedy, she writhed in his arms, driving him wild. He hoisted her higher and forced her harder against the wall, pressing against her breasts, stomach, and hips to hold her still. Kneading the soft skin of her breast, Miguel scraped his thumb across the nipple. Then he took her lips again in a hard kiss, sweeping the sensitive roof of her mouth with the tip of his tongue. They devoured each other, and he angled his head to steal every breath she took.

He was so engrossed he didn't hear the ringing cell phone at first, but eventually it penetrated the fog of his brain. He recognized the familiar sound. The unique ring tone signaled a call from his brother, Aarón.

Their bodies stilled and with great reluctance, he withdrew his mouth from hers. Her complete withdrawal came fast as she unwound herself from around him, and he lowered her to the ground onto her feet.

The insistent chirping of the phone continued.

Miguel needed time to collect himself because he could hardly breathe. Leaning on his forearm, his hand curled into a fist of frustration above her head. He watched as she cut him off by pulling her shirt down to cover her bared breasts.

This couldn't be happening. Not right now.

Samirah looked away from him. With the heavy rise and fall of her chest and lips plumped from kissing, she enticed him, and he thought about turning off the phone and carrying her into the house to finish what they'd started.

The ringing stopped, but before he could say a word, it started up again.

He closed his eyes momentarily. *"No te muevas,"* he said grimly.

Even though he told her not to move, the minute he reached into his pocket for the phone, she slipped under his arm and grabbed her discarded bag.

"I said don't move," he muttered, reaching for her, but only grabbed air. She slipped away, and helplessly, he watched her rush out the gate away from him.

Forcing his voice into neutral, Miguel answered before the voice mail picked up again.

* * *

SAMIRAH TIPTOED into the quiet house. She could smell whatever the Hills had eaten for dinner in the air. She didn't bother to check the refrigerator to see what was left over because food was the last thing on her mind. Quietly, she moved through the house to her quarters and closed the door. Leaning back against it, she let out a heavy breath and lowered her lids. Never had she wanted a man so much. The mere thought of not having him caused a physical ache as basic as hunger or thirst.

Tossing her package on the sofa, Samirah went into the bathroom and took a quick, cold shower. Feeling refreshed, she put on a clean pair of underwear and a tank top she used to sleep in and climbed into bed. She burrowed under the covers, as if they could protect her from her thoughts. The frigid temperature of the water hadn't sufficed. Since the night was still young, maybe she could sleep off her horniness.

Saved by the ring, she thought with disgust. Was she really so weak and impulsive she would have had sex with him? So far she hadn't lived up to any of her promises. She hadn't stayed out of trouble, and she'd come close to having sex.

She'd never run from her sexuality before, but dammit, this trip was about taking a break and getting to know herself better —the opportunity to regroup and assess her life going forward. She wasn't getting any younger and needed to think seriously about her future. She couldn't jaunt across the globe forever. Time to start thinking long term, about serious issues like kids and how she would support herself in her old age.

She thought back to her first experience abroad alone, when she'd decided to do her Le Cordon Bleu externship in Italy. She hadn't slowed down since then, wanting to see the world and visit places other than the Caribbean where most of her maternal family lived. Ten years later, she felt the hankering for something more permanent.

Turning onto her side, she glanced at the clock on the bedside table and realized only a few minutes had passed since she last looked at it. It seemed more like twenty hours.

She tossed again, staring up at the ceiling, and wished she could stop thinking about what had happened between her and Miguel. Now that she'd felt his hands, she couldn't rein in the ideas that trotted through her mind. Her thoughts skittered to the memory of their embrace, of her pinned against the wall as he kissed her. His touch had been so good, so intoxicating, it remained stamped into her psyche like indelible ink.

What would it feel like if he buried his fingers in her hair, yanking her head back to force her to submit to whatever...?

Samirah swallowed and kicked off the sheet in frustration. The night was no warmer than any other since her arrival, but the heat generated by her thoughts made her uncomfortably hot. With trembling fingers that reflected the tumultuous emotions rushing through her, Samirah dragged the tank over her head and tossed it onto the floor in the darkness. Her taut nipples rubbed against the cotton sheets, the torturous friction making her moan until she had to cup her breasts in her soothing palms to ease the throbbing pain.

She just needed to take the edge off, that was all.

She slipped her fingers below the waistband of her panties to stroke the swollen flesh between her legs. They glided through the slick cream, and she pressed her face into the pillow to muffle her moans. Panting, she worked her hips, imagining Miguel touching her, getting her off, stroking her just right with his long fingers.

"Oh," she moaned aloud.

She clutched her breast and pinched the nipple between her fingers, on the very breast he'd tortured with his thumb. She continued to stroke and apply pressure between her legs. The mounting tension made her pants come harsher and faster. Release came hard, flooding her body in pleasure. Squeezing her eyes tight, she let out a loud gasp, turning her head to groan into the pillow as she grinded her hips against her palm.

Her heart rate slowed. Sliding her hand from between her thighs, she rolled onto her back. Hair clung to her sweat-dampened neck, but she could breathe a little easier. Maybe now she could sleep.

Now she could think clearly. Tomorrow she would focus on her future and forget about the sexy Latino next door. In the morning, she would work on her plans for her restaurant. She'd already had an idea of the colors and table settings she would use. Miguel would not become a distraction. She needed to focus—and stay the hell away from him.

* * *

MIGUEL PACED the floor of his dark bedroom. His brother had told him their mother hinted about a move to Europe with her

German boyfriend. Aarón didn't want to go and asked if he could come live with Miguel if she decided to move.

"Of course," he'd assured his brother. But he knew the final decision was their mother's, and he doubted she would be receptive to turning over her eleven-year-old son to him.

Patricia Delgado had a bad track record when it came to men. He could still remember the day his father walked out on them. He hadn't understood the enormity of it at the time, but when his father left, he took the only means of income for him and his mother. Hearing her tears at night had saddened him, but what could a five-year-old do?

By the time he turned eight, his mother had found a new way to support them. At the time, he hadn't fully understood what the string of men passing in and out of their one bedroom apartment meant, but the older kids in the neighborhood did.

They teased him mercilessly, calling his mother names. One night, when she had one of her "friends" over and he was lying on the couch, he turned the TV down. He could hear them, though he knew she tried to be quiet.

Unable to stand it anymore, he had gone to the door and knocked, wiggling the doorknob, begging her to come out. He'd promised to get a job.

"Mama," he'd sobbed, "stop. Please. I'll take care of you." He hadn't even understood what he was asking her to stop. He only knew it was bad.

After the man left, she scolded and spanked him and said, "I'm doing this for us." She told him to never interrupt her when she was working again.

Coming back to the present, Miguel sank onto the edge of the bed and buried his face in his hands. She'd upgraded the type of men she got involved with, but the situation remained more or less the same. And even though he'd offered to take care of her, she'd refused.

What kinds of things did Aarón see or hear? Did he understand the trade his mother made with her body in exchange for dubious security with one man after another?

He couldn't let his brother go through what he did. Convincing his mother would not be easy, but he would do whatever he could to keep Aarón from the same destructive path he'd gone down for years before he'd found a male figure to mentor him.

CHAPTER 7

*A*fter handing over their invitations to the young woman standing at the door, Thomas and Samirah entered the exhibit hall for the art fundraiser arm-in-arm. Samirah held onto him for dear life, worried she would twist her ankle, or worse, take a tumble in front of everyone because she had foolishly decided to wear shoes with such high, skinny heels, making her feel like she teetered several feet up on a pair of stilts. Every step was made carefully, like walking a tight rope.

"Are you sure you'll be all right, my dear?" Thomas asked with a worried frown.

"Yes," Samirah assured him. "Just don't leave my side tonight."

Thomas looked dashing with his silver hair neatly combed and wearing a black tuxedo with satin lapels and a bowtie. On the ride over, Samirah made him blush when she told him he cleaned up well and she'd definitely have to keep an eye on him for Geneva.

A low murmur of conversation floated throughout the room. Photographers circulated among the well-dressed attendees. Their cameras flashed every now and again as they took pictures of the works of art and candid shots of the guests.

Behind three cloth-covered tables stood six young people dressed in white shirts and black slacks serving the food and appetizers covering the tables. Samirah deduced they were students who had volunteered their services for the event. Matted and framed student-donated paintings and sketches covered the walls, turning the space into a temporary art gallery. Display cases sat atop stands, showcasing handmade jewelry, pottery, and sculptures.

In the middle of the room and in front of the stage, clearly the star of the show, sat a large alabaster sculpture of a woman holding a boy in her arms. Samirah and Thomas joined the others who stood around admiring it.

The woman in the sculpture sat on a stool, cradling a young boy in what seemed to be a comforting embrace. The level of detail was so remarkable Samirah could see the creases in their clothes and even the eyelashes lying against the mother's cheek. It seemed at any moment life could be breathed into the inanimate object and the mother and son would get up and join the party.

"Lovely, isn't it?" Thomas said.

"It *is* amazing," Samirah agreed.

"If I didn't know better, I'd say that was a Delgado."

At the mention of Miguel's name, Samirah's heart lurched in her chest. "Was he supposed to donate one of his works for the auction?"

"No, but perhaps he did."

"It is a Delgado," a man in front of them said in a thick Spanish accent. He turned sideways so they had a better view of the sculpture. Pointing to the base, he said, "See his signature? There is a rumor he will make an appearance tonight." He sounded like an excited child who couldn't wait to open gifts on Christmas morning.

"Splendid!" Thomas said. "This piece will raise so much money for the arts."

"Mhmm." Samirah's gaze darted around the room. Miguel should be easy to spot because of his height, but she didn't see anyone who looked remotely like him.

Avoiding him had turned out to be much easier than expected. A taxi pulled up to his house on Thursday morning, and he left with a duffle bag. She hadn't seen any activity at the house since then.

Fifteen minutes later, she and Thomas strolled into a smaller room to view the abstract sculptures made from everyday items and scrap metal. As they made their way back into the main room, she asked Thomas if he'd decided on a piece to purchase.

"I think I'd like the one on the wall over there." He pointed to a mixed media piece comprised of paint, paper, and aluminum. "Or the collage over there."

"You'd better get a numbered paddle if you plan to bid on those."

He nodded his agreement. "Will you be all right if I leave you alone?"

Samirah smiled. "I'll stay close to this wall in case I lose my balance, so I'll have something to hold onto." Concern clouded his face. "I'm kidding. Go."

As the night wore on, Samirah became comfortable with the idea that Miguel would not attend the event. He must still be out of town. A small amount of disappointment surfaced, but she squashed it. She didn't need him hanging around, distracting and tempting her.

She and Thomas stood with another couple, enjoying nibbling on appetizers, when a commotion near the entryway into the grand hall caught her attention. A small crowd had gathered and a series of flashes burst from the cameras of the onlookers. She didn't have to see the man to know who had arrived, but she caught sight of him through the crowd anyway.

He looked even better than when she'd last seen him. Like Thomas, Miguel wore a tuxedo, but he filled his out in way Thomas didn't. The ivory vest and matching tie contrasted against the black of the open tuxedo jacket. His dark hair hung loosely around his ears, and when he looked up, their gazes connected across the room. Her stomach quivered a welcome and memories of their short, hot embrace crashed through her mind.

* * *

MIGUEL HAD ENTERED the exhibit hall after a brief meeting with his former mentor, Esteban Callas, the head of the art department at the University of Cuenca. The day before he had flown to Guayaquil to participate in the afternoon session of a conference. He and other artists spoke to government officials about the importance of the arts and how to revive the Las Peñas neighborhood in the city of Guayaquil. In the 1960's it had been a thriving artist community with regular exhibitions. Now it mainly served as a tourist attraction for those who wanted a view from Santa Ana Hill or liked to visit the old homes there. Major changes would be needed, but they could only be achieved through cooperative efforts between the government and locals.

When Esteban had asked him to donate a sculpture for tonight's event, he readily agreed, but delayed confirming whether or not he could attend because he wasn't sure he'd get back in time. Standing with his hand in his pocket, he fielded questions from the people who circled him, reminded of why he shunned the spotlight. He seldom took photos, and living in a small city like Cuenca provided him with a certain level of anonymity he treasured.

He watched as Samirah returned her attention to the conversation with Thomas, but not before he could drink in the vision she made in the bold-colored dress. On anyone else, it would have been out of place amid the conservative attire of the other women at the venue, but not on Samirah. In fact, she would have looked out of place if she had worn a boring color like black.

He noted how other men cast surreptitious glances in her direction. Her shiny, black hair was swept atop her head in a loose twist—looking easy enough to undo with the tug of a finger. A golden array of bracelets encircled her small wrists, and the earrings she'd purchased at the boutique glittered in her ears.

Unable to stand it any longer, he muttered an excuse to the people around him, intending to make his way over to her.

Esteban came into his line of vision. "Are you ready?"

Miguel had agreed to give a brief speech before the auction began. Resigned, he nodded, cast one more glance in Samirah's direction, and followed the older man to the stage. After the introduction, he took over the microphone.

"Good evening," he said in Spanish. "Thank you for coming tonight. It's both an honor and a privilege for me to attend this event and give back to my community."

"Thank you for coming!" a female voice yelled from the audience, which prompted laughs and a round of applause.

Miguel lifted his hand to quiet the crowd.

"I appreciate your enthusiasm," he said with a smile. "As I said, it's a privilege for me to be here. Before I became an artist, I had a very rocky start as a young man. Were it not for this man —" He gestured in the direction of Esteban. "I don't know where I would be. As a teenager, he kept me out of trouble, and he showed me how to channel my energies into more positive pursuits. Without him, we would not be able to have this event here tonight, and very likely, I would not be here before you as Delgado, the sculptor. Please, give a round of applause to the faculty chair and my mentor, Dr. Esteban Callas."

A loud round of applause broke out.

When the clapping died down, Miguel launched into his prepared speech about the importance of supporting the arts and their relevance in society. Drawing on his own experience, he pointed out how as a youth, he'd gotten into and out of trouble. Esteban caught him defacing public property with graffiti one day. Instead of calling the police, he told him he had real talent. If he agreed to remove what he'd done, Esteban said he would show him how to create acceptable images.

Through his encouragement and guidance, Miguel developed a love of creating, rather than destroying. He discovered a love for sculpting, and Esteban funded his first few projects by providing him with sculpting tools and materials. The rest was history.

Tonight's donations would be used to expand art programs in the area—to the benefit of those young people who wanted to pursue careers in art. The money raised would also help local agencies produce more events, shows, and exhibitions to the benefit of all of Cuenca's citizens.

"And so I encourage you to search within your hearts tonight as you consider your bids for these unique pieces from our future artists. Think about the impact each of your dollars will have in our city. Consider the importance of art in our lives —whether it is visual or performance art. Understand that it not only adds beauty to the world around us, but it helps to make us well rounded. It keeps us civilized, and separates us from other living things through the ability to create. Through art, we have a means by which we grow to be better people, and it moves us forward through creativity, the expansion of our imagination, and hope.

"Hope. An important element in dragging a teen out of self-destructive despair. Hope that there would be a better tomorrow, and a young man could live a better life than the one he'd grown used to."

Deafening applause followed when he finished his speech.

Miguel stepped down from the stage and a woman took over to conduct the auction. A few minutes into talking to another guest, he noticed Thomas Hill slowly winding his way through the crowd, a worried expression on his face. Once or twice he stopped and stood on tiptoe, searching for someone.

Miguel excused himself from yet another conversation he'd barely been paying attention to and approached the older man.

"Mr. Hill, is everything all right?" His first thought was that something had happened to Samirah. Since descending the stage, he hadn't seen her, though she'd been easy enough to spot in her red dress when he stood behind the podium.

Thomas Hill seemed surprised Miguel knew his name. "Yes, I mean no. I came here with a young woman—Samirah, but I don't see her. We need to leave immediately. I left my wife alone, and it seems she hurt herself trying to move around without assistance, and now I must hurry home to see to her." He clenched his hands together in worry. "I really, really must go."

Miguel rested a reassuring hand on his arm. "Samirah and I met the other day, so I know who she is. You should go and see to your wife. When I see Samirah, I'll explain to her what happened and make sure she gets home safely."

Thomas's frowning face expressed his reluctance to leave. "I hate to leave her, but…" Miguel didn't have to say another word. Thomas quickly talked himself into a decision. "Please, let her know what happened, and I'll see her at home."

"Of course." Miguel nodded. "I'll explain everything. Don't worry. I'll take care of Samirah."

CHAPTER 8

*S*amirah wiggled her toes one more time before she rose from the padded bench in the ladies' room. Her feet ached like they never had before, and she cursed herself repeatedly for the vanity of buying and wearing these heels. After listening to Miguel's speech, she came into the restroom for a break because all the seats in the main exhibit hall had been taken.

She winced as she squeezed her feet back into the shoes. "How do women wear these things all day?" After a quick check of her face and dress, she exited the restroom.

Back in the main hall, the auction was in full swing. Standing on the outskirts of the crowd, she searched the faces of the attendees but didn't see Thomas anywhere. She did, however, see Miguel talking to another man. During his rousing speech, she'd seen another side of him. The devilish, charming conversationalist had disappeared, replaced with a serious, thoughtful professional who had apparently experienced hardship as a youth.

Samirah wandered away from the crowd assembled before the stage. As the minutes slipped by, she grew concerned because she didn't see Thomas in the group of bidders, nor did she see him among the people still milling about.

Where could he be? In the restroom?

"You look exquisite," a voice said over her left shoulder. Her nipples budded at the sound of his voice, and she closed her eyes for a moment as desire coursed through her veins from his remembered touch.

"Thank you." She could feel him. He was so close.

"Every man in this place wants you." His voice was thick.

"Every man in this place does not want me."

"If they don't, they're blind fools. Every last one of them."

Samirah looked over her shoulder to find Miguel's lowered head close to hers.

"I appreciate the compliment."

"We have unfinished business."

"No, we don't."

He stepped around her, blocking her view of the stage. "Yes, we do." His steady blue gaze rooted her to the spot.

"I'm not going to stand here and argue with you anymore. I don't know how else to tell you I'm not interested."

"Too bad the message from your mouth doesn't match the message your body sends."

Samirah took an unsteady breath, steeling herself for battle against him and her own weak control. "You're one of *those* men. You think my mouth is saying no while my body's saying yes."

"I don't think, *querida*, I know."

Like a chisel, the word chipped away at her protective wall, forcing imaginary pieces to crumble around her. "Don't use that word."

"What word?"

"*Querida*. Don't call me your sweetheart. I'm not."

"You will be before the night is over." His confidence irked her while the upward slant of one corner of his luscious mouth continued to whittle away at her resistance.

"You are unbelievable. What makes you so sure?"

"Because Thomas had to leave you in my care."

"What do you mean Thomas had to leave?"

He explained what had happened, and anger bubbled up inside her. "And you're only now telling me this?"

"I couldn't find you before."

"*You* are not taking me home. If I have to walk barefoot on hot coals all the way back, I'll take the pain."

He gazed down at her lips. "You have such a smart mouth."

She tilted her head to the side. "You say that like it's a bad thing."

"I would love to see what else you can do with this mouth of yours."

Breathe. "You'll never find out."

His gaze narrowed on her. "Yes, you have a very smart mouth. I'm going to have to find something to put in it to keep you quiet." At that moment, she saw the spark in his eyes. The need. The hunger underlying the teasing words. An answering heat unfurled inside of her. "Nothing to say?"

"You took me by surprise." Her voice sounded tight and strained. He didn't play fair, and she was flirting with danger.

"I have many more surprises in store for you, *querida.*"

"You're wasting your time."

"You're so sure?"

"One hundred percent. And you know what else I'm sure about? I'm not staying here another minute. Thomas is gone, and I'm leaving too."

"And who is this lovely young woman?"

* * *

THE HAIRS on the back of Miguel's neck stood up when Esteban approached. He'd been so engrossed in his conversation with Samirah, he hadn't noticed the program was at the halfway mark and a brief intermission.

To his chagrin, Samirah blossomed under the compliment, her eyes filling with pleasure. Extending her hand, she said, "Samirah. Samirah Jamison."

Esteban took her hand. "I do not believe I've ever had the pleasure of meeting you before." To Miguel, he said in Spanish, "Where have you been hiding her?"

"She speaks Spanish," Miguel said in clipped English.

"Even better."

Miguel's attention focused on how the other man's hands remained joined with Samirah's. She laughed, a throaty, sensuous sound that jolted him from his daze. He liked the sound of her laugh, but he wanted it for himself. Had she ever laughed with him? He couldn't remember an instance when she had.

Esteban continued to hold onto her, his larger hands engulfing one of hers, lingering longer than was socially acceptable for new acquaintances.

"Do you plan to hold her hand all night?" His irritated, gruff voice halted their one-on-one conversation like nails on a chalkboard.

They both turned to him. Esteban's eyes filled with surprise, but he let go. "Her hands are so soft, I forgot myself."

Miguel knew very well how soft her hands were. He imagined the rest of her body he hadn't had the good fortune to explore the other night would feel the same way. Right now he needed to get control of the jealousy coursing through him. It was completely unfounded, and out of character when he considered this was his mentor, the man who'd taken him under his wing and been a father to him when he needed direction in his life.

"I hope I will be able to speak to you again before the end of the evening. If not, it was my pleasure." With a gallant bow and a mumbled comment to Miguel, Esteban left the two of them alone.

"You weren't very nice to your friend," Samirah remarked.

"And you were too nice."

"I was being polite, which seems to be a problem for you."

"It's not a problem for me."

"Are you sure about that?"

Miguel stepped closer and bent to her ear. The fragrance of her perfume filled his lungs, tightening the muscles of his neck. He wanted to fill his sheets with the same tantalizing smell. "My problem is with you and the way you smile and flirt with every man who comes within six inches of you."

Her eyes flashed with anger, but behind the flash he saw something else. Had he hurt her with his comment? Too late, he couldn't retract it.

"Flirting? Let me guess, you think I'm flaunting my...assets, too, don't you?" She took a deep breath, fighting to keep her voice low and maintain her composure. "I'm sick and tired of you and everyone else who has a problem with me. Do you know how many times I've heard something similar? Stop. Tone it down. Stop being who I am, right? Because for some reason, it makes *you* uncomfortable." She shook her head. "I don't think so. I'm a social person, and I like making new friends. This is who I am, and I'm not changing for you or anyone else. If you don't like it, too damn bad. It's your problem, not mine."

"Keep your voice down," Miguel said between gritted teeth as a few people nearby turned in their direction.

Despite her obvious anger, she lowered her tone when she spoke again. "Go. To. Hell."

Miguel watched as she wobbled as fast as she could out of the hall. He managed to catch up to her, and when she pushed her way through the exterior double doors, he grabbed her arm before she could get down the stairs to the parking lot.

Samirah snatched her arm out of his grasp. "I'm not staying here another minute, and I mean it. I'm not letting you or anyone else insult me. I'm not a slut, and I'm not a whore."

The tremor in her voice rocked him. "I never called you any of those things."

"No, but you think it. That's why you think I'll have sex with you, but I won't." She cursed and bent down to slip off a shoe.

"What are you doing?"

"What does it look like I'm doing?" she hissed. Off came the other one, and she lost four inches. "My feet are killing me in these horrible shoes, and I knew good and well I shouldn't have bought them in the first place."

"If you knew you shouldn't have bought them," Miguel said, "why did you?"

"Because they went with the dress."

"Why do you women do such things to yourselves?"

"Because of you men!"

Miguel couldn't believe he was standing outside, arguing about shoes, when he couldn't care less about them. He pinched the bridge of his nose, indecisive about whether he should kiss her or throttle her.

It was because of the sassy way she'd put her hand on her hip to give him a piece of her mind, the pout of those full lips, and the way the lights flicked across her skin, inviting him to touch. Each movement called out to him.

"Trust me," he said, enunciating each word. "Most men don't care about what you have on your feet." At least they didn't when a woman was on her back under him. "Now put your shoes on and get back inside, and I'll escort you home when the event is over."

Oh, she didn't like that. Her eyes changed color, spitting fire at him. The hand holding the shoes went back to her hip. "Or what? What are you going to do? Nothing."

She turned away and said something in another language. He didn't know what she said, but he was fairly certain whatever it was, she said it in French. She cursed at him. If he'd even doubted it for a minute, her next act confirmed his thought.

When her foot connected with the bottom step, she lifted her hand and stuck her middle finger in the air. She held her hand upright for a long time and added extra energy to her walk. Daring him to do something.

His eyes narrowed as he watched her walk away—in the red dress he helped pick out. A dress which fit like a second layer of skin on her ripe body. Her perfectly shaped butt cheeks moved up and down beneath the stretchy fabric, her hips rolling as she let them sway side to side like the pendulum on a clock.

His blood boiled as she purposely taunted him, daring him to make a move, like she had that night at Seth's Bar.

Baiting him.

His control snapped like a twig under foot. Her petulant anger shouldn't turn him on, but it did. He wanted to claim her, put his stamp on her.

What are you going to do? Nothing.

Miguel started down the steps.

It was time Samirah Jamison learned a lesson. And he was just the man to teach it to her.

CHAPTER 9

*S*amirah was ill-prepared for what happened next. One minute she was walking away, the next she was thrown over Miguel's shoulder like a piece of rolled carpet.

A startled cry of protest left her lips. "What—what are you doing?" she sputtered. "Put me down!"

"Be quiet." His palm landed squarely on her behind, stinging through the material of her clothes, pushing a gasp past her lips and forcing her squirming body to freeze in shock.

Who the hell did he think he was, hitting her like that? And why did she enjoy it so much?

Her heart pounded beneath her ribs as she realized he was marching away from the building, away from the auction and any type of help she could receive from the attendees.

"I'm going to scream," she threatened.

"I certainly hope so."

"Put. Me. Down."

"If you don't be quiet, I'll put you over my knee and spank you."

"You wouldn't dare! If you hit me again, you'll pull back a stub."

She realized how ridiculous her claims sounded as she hung upside down over his shoulder, clutching her shoes in one hand, but she had to say something to counteract the physical response her body had to his words. She should be indignant that he thought he could get away with putting his hands on her. Instead, the threat of corporal punishment excited her, made her nipples hard and moisture emerge between her thighs.

Miguel hit her again, never breaking stride as he marched between the cars. Samirah bit the inside of her mouth to refrain from moaning. The pulse created by the blow of his hand made her forget to breathe. When she remembered, breath rushed from her lungs. Embarrassingly aroused, she twisted and kicked, struggling to break free from his iron grip.

Her actions proved successful. Miguel dropped her onto her feet between a row of cars. With his fists clenched at his sides, he loomed over her. "You are the most difficult woman I have ever met!"

"Who do you think you are, carrying me off like some kind of caveman?" she fumed.

He shook his head in frustration. "You need to be taught a lesson."

A promise or a threat, she wasn't sure. At the same time, she realized she was so far away from the building that any attempt at screaming would not be heard.

She saw the look in his eyes and knew what he planned to do. Stepping back, she lifted her hand to deflect his actions. "Don't you dare!"

The words fell on deaf ears. With one hand to the back of her exposed nape, he hauled her close and settled his mouth over hers. The shoes clattered to the tarmac from her nerveless fingers. An instant buzz of electricity zoomed through her as he pried her lips apart with the smooth glide of his tongue.

Winding the other arm around her waist, he mashed her to

him, trapping her arms between them while he ravaged her mouth with hungry kisses. He devoured her lips.

Crushed along the length of him, she could hardly breathe. "You drive me out of my mind." He shoved his fingers into her hair and tightened them into a fist.

The resulting pain only aroused her more. Her body quaked —not from fear but from anticipation. She trembled on tiptoe, clawing at the wool of his jacket, impatient for what was to come. He breathed the next words against her neck. "You shake your sexy little *colita* in my face and don't expect me to react?"

With his hand in her hair, he drew her head back at a sharp angle to give him greater access to her throat. She groaned as his hot mouth sucked and kissed, traveling over her skin to the neckline of her dress. "So soft," he rasped. More nibbling and sucking at the crest of her breast, his actions sure to leave a mark.

Her feet disappeared from under her as he lifted her into his arms. She landed on her back with a gasp, knocking the wind from her lungs, her hot skin cooling wherever it touched the hood of the car he deposited her on. The bracelets on her wrists clanked against the metal when her hands landed on either side of her head. He moved fast, his deft fingers undoing the hidden clasp on her shoulder before he lowered his head to her exposed breasts.

He sucked them, forcing the nipples into rigid peaks. His merciless mouth and teeth scraped along the tender flesh while his hands worked their way under her dress.

"Miguel...yes, oh God," she moaned on a pant, clutching the hairs on his head. The need, the hunger was almost unbearable —fueled by anger and unsatisfied lust.

"Are you done running?" he demanded. His pupils were dilated, and an almost feral brilliance filled his eyes. He dragged the scrap of lacy panties down her legs and tossed it away from him. His fingers found the incriminating wetness. Groaning, he fondled her, stroking his fingers across the wet lips between her thighs like they belonged to him.

"Yes." Samirah choked on the word. She closed her eyes, appalled at the impropriety of their actions in the middle of the parking lot where anyone from the event could exit at any moment and see them—see her, sprawled across a stranger's car with her dress folded up to her waist and his hand between her legs.

His fingers sank into her thighs, and he dragged her to the edge of the hood. The loose knot of curls on her head finally fell free. Heat radiated across her skin where he touched, and yearning wound its way through her body, shaming her with its intensity. She didn't even have the strength to stop him. She had no desire to.

The soft grind of a zipper's teeth penetrated the sound of their panting breaths as he undid his pants. He positioned himself between her legs, and she realized he aimed to do the unthinkable—right there, in the middle of the parking lot.

He leaned over her, blocking the glaring lights from the pole nearby. His dark brown hair fell forward and cast his features in shadow. He pushed her knees back to her chest, pinning her down. She felt the broad head of his penis against the entrance to her body. "Now I'll give us what we both want."

The raw timbre of his voice exposed the imbalance of his emotions. He was losing himself, his accent so strong she could barely understand what he said.

He pushed into her with such force, she cried out. Her fingers trembled as she stretched her arms to grab onto his shoulders. Her body twisted and arched in a desperate attempt to accommodate his size.

He withdrew slowly, bathed in the moisture from her body, and powered into her again. A sob of immense pleasure broke from her throat. She moaned, begged, struggled to breathe. Picking up the pace, he groaned, showing no mercy. But she didn't want mercy. She got exactly what she wanted—heart-pounding, incredible sex that made her indifferent to their surroundings.

He restrained her wrists above her head, and with her calves on his shoulders, she couldn't move an inch. All she could do was take the pounding he dished out. His hips slammed against her thighs in quick succession, jouncing her naked breasts, rocking her body with each advance. Over and over. She took it, trembled from the sheer pleasure and force of it, certain he would dent the metal at her back with the strength of each thrust.

The coiled tension in her loins loosened under the onslaught. Above her, his breath grew shallow, fanning her temple. His movements became more urgent as he chased release. Her head tilted back, and her nails bit into her palms. Stars burst behind her eyelids.

The beat of ecstasy pounded through her veins as she gave herself over to such intense pleasure she couldn't hold her screams. It was too good to keep to herself. Her throbbing cries drifted on the night air.

He trembled, gripping her slender wrists in a tight hold as he frantically drove into her harder, faster, and with a mighty roar, found satisfaction.

BEADS OF SWEAT dotted Miguel's forehead. Tendrils of hair clung to his face where his hair had dipped forward across his brow. He eased from between Samirah's legs and silently zipped his trousers while she slid from on top of the vehicle and adjusted her clothes.

Her eyes remained downcast, not looking at him, and how could he blame her? He'd charged into her with the care and finesse of an Iberian bull.

He watched her bend over to pick up her underwear, and his shaft swelled, wanting to get back inside of her.

What was the matter with him?

He uttered a stream of curse words under his breath.

"Samirah." She froze in the midst of stepping into her thong. "I…" What should he say? He didn't regret what happened, just how it happened. He ran the fingers of his hands through his hair, brushing the strands back and away from his face. The wrists of both hands rested on the back of his head. "It wasn't supposed to happen like that."

He'd never been out of control before—wanting a woman so much he took her with such force and gave no thought to protection.

"How was it supposed to happen?" She finished pulling up her underwear with her back to him.

He wanted to touch her, but he worried she would withdraw from him. "Look at me. Please."

Slowly, she faced him and met his gaze. Her hair was a mess of curls on her head and her lips, swollen. She looked so fragile.

"I know I was too rough—"

"No—"

"—but I lost my head. It's no excuse—"

"—you weren't."

He stopped when her words registered. Gazing down into her face, he drank in her delicate features. "What are you saying?"

"I'm fine. You didn't hurt me."

"Still, I should have…" He sighed heavily.

Unable to help himself, he gathered her into his arms. She melted against him. Nuzzling her neck, he inhaled deeply and kissed her fragrant skin. His fingers gathered a handful of curls while the other hand stroked down her bare arm then around to her back.

"You should go back inside," she whispered, easing out of his arms. "They'll be looking for you."

When she pulled away, it felt as if someone cut off his arm. "I'm not going back inside. I'm taking you home."

"I can catch a cab on my own."

"It's not up for debate." No more words needed to be spoken.

He took her hand in his and led the way off the grounds. They walked in silence out to the street where he hailed a taxi. All the way back, they sat on opposite ends of the seat. When they arrived at their destination, she stepped out of the vehicle. He handed the driver a bill and didn't bother waiting for change because she was walking away and he couldn't let her leave.

By the time she rounded the front of the taxi, he was two steps ahead of her. "I'll take my time," he said.

She looked confused, not knowing what he was talking about. The spoken words were part of a conversation he'd been having in his head on the ride over. They stood in the middle of the street, and he started backing her toward the gate. "I can't let you go tonight," he whispered in a rough undertone.

His hand was already under her dress again, coasting up the thigh exposed by the split. He captured her shallow breaths with a kiss to her bruised lips. "I can't. Not yet." His fingers reached the apex of her thighs and fingered the edge of her panties at the crease of her hips.

She inhaled sharply, parting her legs so he could touch her more intimately. One arm snaked around his neck and he drew her closer, kissing harder.

When he lifted his head to look down at her, she gave him a sensual look from beneath half-lowered lids. "I have to taste every inch of you tonight," he whispered, brazenly caressing the bare cheeks of her bottom.

His desire for her knew no bounds. He wanted her now, with her back against the gate, for all of their neighbors to see.

Anywhere, anytime. Public or private. He couldn't imagine not wanting her.

With no hesitation, he lifted her in his arms and took her inside his house. He set her on her feet before his mouth covered hers again. The shoes in her hands thumped when they hit the carpet. She caught his face between her palms and opened her sweet mouth to him. The kiss started slow but morphed into a heated tangle of tongues.

She relieved him of his jacket, and with feverish kisses and roaming hands, they stumbled toward the staircase. Halfway up, she lost her panties.

He caressed her hips, her thighs, her breasts, while she smoothed her hands up his chest and pressed her soft body against him.

In the hallway, his vest and tie came off and her bracelets and earrings dropped on top of them.

When they entered the bedroom, the open curtains offered enough light for them to finish undressing, and he wasted no time getting her on her back.

* * *

HIS MOUTH TRAVELED over the crest of her breast and pulled the nipple into his mouth. The sight of his tanned skin against her darker skin aroused Samirah even further. He sucked them with such utter enjoyment, curled over her, caging her in with the length and width of his large body.

He filled his hands with her breasts, kneading the soft mounds, squeezing them together as he licked and sucked the skin of her ribs and made his way down her stomach to the sensitive flesh of her thighs.

Even in her delirious state, Samirah registered that he reached into a drawer in his nightstand and placed several condoms on top of it. Once sheathed in protection, he slid into the slick wetness of her body.

"You feel incredible," he whispered raggedly. *"Dime lo que quieres."*

How could she tell him what she wanted when her brain cells had ceased to function over an hour ago? "Please, please," she whispered.

She'd learned to say "give it to me harder" and all sorts of vulgar things in four languages, and yet with this man, she reverted back to senseless muttering in her mother tongue.

Samirah angled her pelvis up, taking him as deep as he could go. She tweaked her nipples, further heightening her arousal as she undulated her hips in time to his movements. His pace picked up as he watched her. She put on a show for him, massaging her breasts, moaning, ratcheting up the heat between them.

He muttered a flurry of Spanish and lowered his head to lick at her nipples in the spaces between her fingers—as if his tongue was jealous of her hands.

It was so decadent, so delicious to feel the contrast of sensations—the moist slip of his tongue and the pressure of her hands on her own breasts—that it triggered an explosion within her body, her inner muscles tightening around him like a fist.

He took advantage of her trembling body, raised her leg, and placed the sole of her foot flat against his chest. The scissorslike position provided deep, sensational penetration. Her hypersensitive body came alive again as he slipped in and out of her with rapid, urgent thrusts.

Shuddering contractions racked her body once more, and with an uttered groan he found his own release.

CHAPTER 10

*S*amirah woke slowly. The veil of sleepiness eventually fell away and she remembered where she was. Her gaze traveled around what she could see of Miguel's bedroom.

White walls with no pictures. White curtains. White dresser. No color anywhere, even on the bed where she lay under white sheets.

She lifted onto her elbow and peered over her shoulder at his sleeping form. Her breath hitched in her throat at his masculine beauty. He lay on his side, and his tousled, dark hair half covered one side of his face. Morning stubble shadowed his chin and jaw, adding a decidedly roguish look that added to his appeal. One muscular arm draped across her hip, and the sculpted lips that had kissed her so passionately last night appeared relaxed but just as tempting.

How to get away without waking him up?

Samirah eased toward the edge of the bed, using the smallest movements she could. Behind her she heard him grunt and turn. She halted, holding her breath. When she looked over her shoulder again, she saw he now lay sprawled on his back. His even breathing indicated he still slept.

Without him touching her, it made getting out of the bed easier, but she moved stealthily so as not to disturb him further. In front of the dresser, she assessed her appearance and grimaced. She had a passion mark above her right breast and on the inside of her right thigh. Faint bruises encircled her wrists from when he'd pinned her to the top of the car. She turned her back to the mirror and ran a fingertip over the reddish marks on her butt cheek left behind by his teeth.

What was left of her curls was flattened against one side of her head. She did what she could with her fingers before looking for her dress. It lay against the wall in a crumpled red heap.

"Where do you think you're going?"

Samirah bolted upright, clutching the dress in front of her. He looked across at her from a relaxed pose against the pillows. "Home."

"Why?"

"I figured we were done here."

He yawned, stretching. "It's Saturday."

"So?"

"It's your day off." He sat up in the bed.

"I can still go home."

His eyes assessed her as she stood close to the wall, clutching her dress to her naked body as if it could protect her from him. "Come back to bed," he said calmly.

"Does that work with other women? Because I don't appreciate being spoken to like I'm a child."

"Then stop acting like one. Get back in this bed."

"Last night was good, okay? Is that what you want to hear? I just need to go home and...and..."

He simply had to let her go, because she needed to get home and figure out what the hell was happening to her. Why she felt so...vulnerable. As if she would fall apart at any minute. Vulnerability was a foreign emotion to her. She didn't like it at all.

If she entered into an affair with Miguel, she knew she would never be whole again because whenever they ended their relationship, a piece of her would remain behind with him.

It wouldn't be like when she lost her virginity to her brother's bad boy frat brother who broke the rules: no sisters, ex-wives, baby mommas, or ex-girlfriends. It wouldn't even be like when she *thought* she'd lost her heart to her boss at the restaurant in Miami.

With Miguel, she *knew* she would lose her heart. Such was the danger he presented—a danger she'd recognized when they met at Seth's Bar only days ago. An affair with him wouldn't be casual because she risked losing a part of herself.

He rose from the bed with graceful ease, unashamed in all his nakedness. "It's Saturday. You owe me a meal, remember, for not telling your employers that you were using my pool without permission. And I'm looking forward to more of what we shared last night." He continued to speak in a calm voice, as if he were telling her to stop at the store to get milk.

"I need to take a shower," she mumbled as he prowled closer, pressing backward against the wall, hoping to disappear within it. "I—I need clean clothes. I need underwear."

He reached her and electricity sizzled across the small space separating them. One hand came to rest on the wall above her head. His light blue eyes looked steadily down into her brown ones.

"You can take your shower here, and you can wear one of my shirts." With his other hand, he reached up and eased the dress from her death grip and dropped it at their feet. "And don't worry about underwear. You won't be needing any today." He scooped her up into his arms. "Time for your shower."

Samirah looked into his eyes and brushed the dark, sleep-rumpled hair back from his forehead. Her stomach tightened, and she buried her face in his neck. How could she resist when he smelled good—like the morning air, good sex, and all man?

Whipped. That's what she was—after one night. She was already in too deep, falling for him fast and hard. She knew it just as sure as she knew her own name. All she could do now was enjoy her time with him—with the understanding that her heart wouldn't recover when it was time to let go.

* * *

HOURS LATER, Samirah descended the stairs in search of Miguel. She wore one of his long-sleeved, button-down shirts. After their shower together, they'd made love again. Then they took a nap, after which Miguel left her upstairs and returned thirty minutes later with a tray laden with a breakfast they ate together before tumbling once more into each other's arms.

When she rolled out of bed, the clock said twenty minutes after twelve. She'd already called to check on Geneva and let her and Thomas know she was fine. They didn't question her whereabouts but expressed their appreciation for checking in.

On the first floor, Samirah found the kitchen empty. She sauntered through the house, noting the same sterile décor as upstairs. White or gray everywhere and nothing on the walls. In the living room she stopped in front of a table displaying a few photographs. One in particular caught her eye. It was a picture of Miguel and a young boy of about eight or nine who bore a striking resemblance to him. The boy stood holding a baby crocodile up to the camera, and Miguel stood behind him, smiling. She recognized the spot as Bayside Marketplace in Miami. She even knew the vendor who people paid to take photos with his baby crocodile, snake, and iguanas.

Did Miguel have a son?

She realized she knew so little about him, and she wanted to know more.

Continuing her search, she found him in the back of the house. The entire length of the back half of it had been transformed into a large studio. Several unfinished sculptures were spaced throughout the room. She stood in the doorway, watching him work. Shirtless and wearing a pair of worn jeans, he sat hunched over a sculpture in relief, a raised image of one of Cuenca's most famous buildings, the New Cathedral of Cuenca. Using sand paper, he smoothed the edges and used a fine brush to disperse the dust particles.

"Come in," he called without looking up.

She entered. "I didn't want to disturb you."

He looked up at her, his gaze running down her body and settling on her exposed legs.

"You're not disturbing me. I'm almost finished." He returned to the task.

A rolling table with his tools sat within reach. She recognized a chisel, a wooden mallet, and a knife, but there were other sharp-looking instruments she didn't know the names of. She guessed they were used to make more intricate cuts in the plaster for things like eyelashes.

The desire to reach for him filled her, to slide her hands across the smooth muscles of his back and trace the middle of his spine with the tip of her forefinger, maybe drop a tender kiss on his back. The affectionate gesture would no doubt be seen as too familiar—ridiculous considering everything they'd done to each other upstairs.

To take her mind off touching him, Samirah scrutinized the room further. Fifty-pound bags of plaster were stacked in a corner. There was also a sink for washing up and three buckets in a line against one wall.

She stepped over to a window and pulled aside the curtain to look out into the backyard and realized he might have been working in here when he saw her in the pool.

"Do you ever paint your sculptures?"

"Rarely. Most people want them just the way I create them, with no embellishments. If I did paint them, there's more work involved. I have to seal the plaster first before I paint over it."

"What are the buckets for?"

"To mix the plaster in with water." She heard him roll back on the stool and she turned in his direction to see him go to the sink to wash his hands.

"How long does it take for the plaster to dry?"

"Once I slap it on the frame," he said, drying his hands, "I leave it overnight to set."

He reclaimed his seat. "Any more questions?" Amusement filled his eyes.

She saw an opportunity to learn more about him. Emboldened, Samirah went to him. He smiled up at her. She let her thumb trace the scar above his left eye. "How did you get this?"

The smile on his face vanished, and his fingers closed around her wrist. He held her gaze so long she thought he wouldn't answer, and she feared she'd crossed some invisible line of demarcation.

"I was in a fight," he finally said.

"It must have been some fight."

"I barely remember it."

She shook her head, determined to make him tell her. "I don't believe you. I think you remember it very well."

His mouth set in a grim line, and then he rose abruptly from the chair to walk over to the same window she'd stared out of. Silence stretched between them for some time. "I was in a fight when I was twelve. A boy said something ugly about my mother. He called her a whore."

Samirah gasped. "Why would he call her that?"

He laughed, but there was no amusement in it. "Because she was. She slept with men for money. It started after my father left us, and it continued for a long time until she figured out a better way to get the lifestyle she wanted." The deadpan tone of voice didn't fool Samirah. It hid a multitude of hurt. "It wasn't the first time kids had said ugly things about my mother, but that day"—he shook his head—"*that day*, I'd had enough, and I decided I wouldn't put up with it any longer. We fought, cheered on by a small group of kids in the neighborhood. When he realized he was losing, he smashed a bottle and came at me."

Samirah lifted her hand to her mouth, horrified at what had happened to him.

"He cut me right here." He fingered the scar. "The blood scared him and the other kids, and possibly saved my life. They ran off and left me there on the ground, with blood streaming down my face. An adult came along and took me to the hospital. The other boy never bothered me again. I guess it's true what they say about standing up to bullies."

Samirah padded over to him on the dusty floor. She wanted to wrap her arms around him. Instead, she said, "I'm so sorry."

He looked down at her. "For what?"

"For what happened to you." Her heart grieved for him.

"It happened a long time ago."

"Yeah, I know. You barely remember it, right?"

He slipped his arm around her neck and drew her closer. "You ask too many questions."

"And you don't ask enough."

"Will I ever get the last word with you?"

"No."

He threw his head back and laughed. The sound warmed her insides and brought a smile to her lips, glad she could make him laugh despite the sadness of the tale he just shared. "Samirah, Samirah," he said, rubbing her back. "You're one of a kind."

"True. I've never met anyone else like me."

"In all the places you've been? I believe you said...what did you say? You're a citizen of the world?"

"I am."

"And where have you been?" He lowered his body to the window sill and rested his hands on her hips.

"Where haven't I been would be easier to tell you." She grew excited. She loved to talk about her travels. "I've been all over, but I've spent most of my time in Europe, Africa, and the Caribbean. This is only my second trip to South America. The first time I came for fun—a trip to Brazil for Carnival."

"You travel from place to place on a whim?"

Samirah shrugged. "Sometimes it's a short vacation, but most of the time, I have a job lined up before I go. It's exciting. Sometimes I'll go somewhere, without a job, and travel around until the money runs out. This world is so big. Why would you want to stay in the same place when you can go anywhere you want? There's so much to see and do. I've run with the bulls in Pamplona, I've danced down the street in Rio's Carnival, I've been to the top of the Eiffel Tour, and I've been to the dungeons of Goree Island. I've seen the Pyramids, and I visited Buckingham Palace. I've seen so much, and there's still plenty I have to see. And in case you're wondering, I speak four languages besides English."

"I wasn't," he teased.

She ignored him. "French, Portuguese, Spanish, and Italian. My Arabic's rudimentary, and right now almost nonexistent, but I could probably pick up the basics again if I had to. A friend got me a job on a military base in Kuwait a few years back, which I then turned into a gig in Dubai. That's how I learned a little Arabic."

"Do you ever want to stop and live somewhere permanently?"

Samirah trailed her fingers down the corded strength of his forearm. "One day," she admitted quietly. "I'd like to own a restaurant." Only her closest family knew about her dream.

"What kind of restaurant?"

"Caribbean-Latin fusion. A combination of the food I learned to cook from my mother and Latin food, which I love."

"There are some common elements in the cuisine. I can see how a menu like that would work."

Pleased he didn't think her idea was silly or unrealistic, Samirah added, "One day, I'll have it, and I'll be my own boss. It'll probably be in Miami, in a trendy part of town. If I could afford it, I'd love to have it on South Beach, where all the action is. I'll be in control of the menu, and no one can dictate whether or not I have a job. I'll make my own future."

"You sound as if you've thought this through in detail."

"I have. I keep a notebook with all of my ideas, and in a couple of years, I'll do it. And the next time you're visiting Miami, you can stop by and have a meal on the house." A grin widened across her face.

Something shifted in his eyes. "I'll take you up on that offer."

"How often do you visit Miami?"

"Not often, but my mother and younger brother live there. My brother's very young. My mother said he was unexpected."

"You don't believe her."

His expression became guarded, as if he'd said too much. "My mother seldom does anything that doesn't benefit her. My brother is only eleven. At the time of his birth, his father was seventy-five."

"Is he the boy in the picture at Bayside Marketplace?" She remembered Geneva mentioned once that he had a little brother.

"Yes."

"Do you—"

"No more questions." He started to undo the buttons on the shirt. "How often can I see you?"

"My contract requires me to stay at the house during the week. But I'm free on the weekends, and I can see you on Karaoke Night."

"It's not enough, but it will have to do."

When the buttons were all open, he pushed the shirt off her

shoulders and drew her closer to latch his mouth onto her breast. His tongue stroked lazily around the circumference of her nipple, forcing her stomach muscles to tighten into a sharp twist of desire.

He palmed the smooth globes of her bottom. "I like you naked."

"I like to be naked."

So what if she'd broken her no man/no sex rule? It was her rule to break. She was hungry for him. There had been a power shift—one she'd never experienced before.

Samirah lowered to her knees on the hard floor. She wanted to taste him—every long, salty inch. When he recognized her intention, the bulge in his jeans grew larger, stretching the denim fabric to capacity.

She popped open the clasp and unzipped the jeans. At the sight of his magnificent erection, she kissed the tip. It twitched at the same time Miguel drew a sharp breath. With her eyes locked with his, Samirah dragged her tongue from the base to the tip and pulled him into her mouth.

MIGUEL SHOVED his fingers into her hair, watching beneath lowered lids as her beautiful lips stretched around his wide shaft and she sucked him in farther. Deeper still, and he muttered an oath at the velvet strokes of her tongue and the warm suction of her mouth. Just when he thought he couldn't experience any more pleasure, he felt the vibrations in the back of her throat.

His head hit the window pane, and he grabbed a handful of her hair. He tried to prolong the tumble into oblivion, but she was too good—a master with her hand and mouth. He ejaculated, pumping his hips through the agony of release.

When she'd sucked him dry, Miguel got shakily to his feet

and dragged her with him. Gripped by an unfamiliar emotion, he kissed her, hard. He planted his large hands on her generous bottom and massaged until her knees weakened so the only thing holding her upright was his hold on her. He pulled her up against him, up onto her toes, and ground his hips into hers, letting her feel how hard he was again. She shivered and grabbed his shoulders to maintain her balance.

"When you're not at work, you'll be with me."

He didn't wait for a reply. It wasn't a request. It was a demand. He kissed her again, taking her acquiescence. With his hands beneath her hips, he lifted her higher until her legs coiled around his waist.

He'd had enough of work. There were more important things to tend to. He marched toward the staircase with her wrapped around him.

They spent the rest of the afternoon in bed.

CHAPTER 11

*M*iguel sat on the wheeled stool downstairs in his studio. With controlled movements, he tapped the mallet to the top of the chisel and began the process of forming a head out of the block of plaster.

Over the past month, he and Samirah spent every moment they could together. Their comfortable routine consisted of fixing breakfast together on Saturday morning and then making love. Afterward, he worked in the studio and she took off to the market to buy groceries for their weekend meals.

Saturday evenings, they ate dinner at his house, went to the movies, or rode the motorcycle into town to listen to music at Parque Calderon. On Sundays, they returned to the park to people watch. Families dominated then, picnicking or playing games. In fact, from time to time, Samirah would join in a game of soccer, and no one ever refused her. Who could?

He thought back to the time he took her to one of the neighboring towns to purchase souvenirs for her family. She ended up also purchasing the traditional colorful skirts of one of the *chola* women for herself. When they arrived back at his place, she put on the two skirts, layered over each other the way the women did.

"Look at the colors!" she'd exclaimed with a twirl. "They're so pretty. I couldn't wait to put them on."

Before he could stop himself, he'd whispered they were nowhere near as beautiful as she. With a mischievous grin, she'd told him to show her just how beautiful he thought she was, and he'd chased her up the stairs, her laughter trailing backward to curl around him and tighten his chest. He could never grow tired of that laugh.

Then there was the time when they'd returned one Saturday night and she stripped out of her clothes and jumped into the pool, screeching at the cold temperature of the water. At first, he'd protested against her invitation to follow suit.

"Come on, Miguel, join me," she'd insisted.

He couldn't resist as he watched her. The moonlight bathed her skin and reflected off the dark surface of the water. Within minutes, he tore out of his clothes and joined her. And within minutes, their slippery wet bodies were joined together as she straddled him on a patio chair.

He even found himself reaching for her hand in public, kissing her in public. Doing things normally reserved for the private moments alone. Like on Karaoke Night, he waited for her at the back of the bar. When she descended the stage and made her way back to him, he would pull her into his arms and kiss her for everyone to see that she was his. If he was fortunate enough to find a seat, he made sure she sat on his lap all night.

He didn't even know himself anymore. He was changing, engaging in activities he normally didn't. If he wasn't careful, she'd soon have him on stage singing, too.

The mallet connected with the chisel with force, and he knocked off a piece that was too big. He swore in frustration. He should stop because he couldn't concentrate.

Miguel rose from the chair. She should be out of her shower already. Her trip to the market would have to be delayed today.

He left the studio and passed by the vase of flowers on the table in the living room. Every week when she went into town, Samirah brought back fresh flowers from the flower market. Over the sofa, she'd had him frame and hang one of the colorful fabrics purchased during a trip to a different town nearby.

When he walked into the bedroom, he could hear her off-key singing in the shower. He opened the door and went in, walking right up to the glass door before she noticed him.

"Hey, what are you doing in here?"

Smiling, he slid open the door. "I wanted to make sure you didn't need any help." He rested his shoulder against the enclosure, admiring the way the tiny streams of water raced down her back and over the curve of her pert bottom.

"You, *señor*, are not here to help, and if I needed any help, I would have called you."

He could take her right now, he was so hard. Despite the amount of time they spent together, it never seemed to be enough. She came over every weekend, and after she went to the market for the Hills on Tuesdays and Thursdays, she spent time with him in the afternoon until she had to go back to the house to fix dinner.

Watching her leave every Sunday evening grew harder with each passing week. He wanted to demand that she remain with him. She was entrenched in his home, and that wasn't supposed to happen. They were supposed to be having a good time, enjoying each other for the short period she was in the country. But now he had a hard time imagining his life without her in it.

The intense nature of his thoughts shocked him. So much so he didn't realize Samirah had turned off the shower and was drying off with a towel until she spoke.

"Hey, did I lose you?" She wrapped the towel around her

body and hung the shower cap inside the stall. Walking right up to him with a grin on her face, she whispered, "Earth to Miguel."

His heart pounded a fierce beat in his chest. Something was wrong here. Very wrong. "I'm fine. My mind wandered for a minute." He kissed her upturned lips.

"Want to talk about it?"

The concern in her voice twisted through him. He wanted to reassure her, yet at the same time, he had to admit the problem that needed to be sorted out lay with him. Samirah was not the kind of woman he saw himself in a long term relationship with. Aside from the fact she would be leaving in a few weeks, he recognized that she could never truly be happy here.

How long would it be before she got bored and moved on? The memory of her words mocked him.

...a citizen of the world. Why would you want to stay in the same place when you can go anywhere you want?

His throat tightened to repress the emotion churning inside him. This casual affair suddenly didn't seem so casual. "Everything's fine."

Skepticism filled her eyes. "If you want to talk, I'm all ears." She moved into the bedroom. He watched her pick up a jar of lotion and dip in her fingers.

Talk. Right.

Talking solved nothing.

He first learned that lesson at the age of fifteen when his mother had decided to move to Colombia with her first "sponsor." He had talked to her, told her he didn't want to go. Her response had been to tell him he could come with her or stay there. He'd stayed behind. Fortunately, he was big for his age, and he found construction work to earn money. He'd slept on couches of friends and family before he finally earned enough to get a small place of his own.

His second lesson on talking came at the age of twenty when

he fell in love with a senior at the university. He had met her through Esteban, and they'd been living together for a year when she told him she wanted to move to New York where she had family and hoped to find success with her art. By then, his sculptures were garnering national attention. He asked her to stay, promised to take care of her. She agreed and stayed for awhile, but eventually, she, too, left—seeking excitement elsewhere.

Samirah smoothed scented cream onto her arms. The towel dropped and she filled her hands with more lotion and rubbed it down over her full breasts, stroking over her stomach, firm butt, and then down to her thighs. She bent over in front of him to get her ankles and feet.

He walked up behind her in slow motion. Her provocative movements sent a charge through him. He'd never met a woman like her before, so confident in her sexuality, and yet with such a sweet disposition that people flocked to her in droves. Everyone in the neighborhood knew her. Her mastery of the Spanish language endeared her all the more to what he could only call her legion of fans. Whenever she walked down the street, they waved and called out her name. He'd lived here for years and only knew a handful of his neighbors. If they knew he was a famous sculptor, they didn't show it.

Her easy assimilation into the day-to-day of Ecuadorian life showed her respect for the culture and made it seem as if she belonged here. *But she doesn't*, he thought. No matter how much it seemed she fit in, when her job was over, she would leave.

Samirah reached behind her with the container. "Would you do my back?"

He brushed her long hair over her shoulder out of the way and then took the jar. He smeared the fragrant substance between his palms and began to smooth it over her skin. The room became charged from the innocent but erotic motions.

"I want to take you somewhere before your contract is up," he said, his voice already getting tight.

"Where?" she breathed.

"The Galapagos Islands."

"I would love to go." She glanced over her shoulder at him. "When?"

"In a couple of weeks. How many days can you get off?"

"I don't know. A few days, maybe."

"You smell so good," he muttered, temporarily distracted. "Your skin is so soft." He lowered his lips to the back of her neck.

"This is what you really came up here for, isn't it?" she whispered breathlessly.

His hand drifted across her stomach and pulled her closer. "*Soy culpable*," he said, admitting his guilt.

She tipped her head back for his kiss. "I have an idea for how we can convince the Hills to give me the time off."

"Tell me later," Miguel said, turning her in his arms so she faced him. He cupped her face in his hands. "But I don't want you to worry about a thing regarding the trip. This will be my gift to you."

He lowered his head to indulge in an earth-shattering kiss before they fell onto the bed. With gentle kisses, he worked his way down her body. Her fingers encouraged him, tangling in the silken threads of his hair.

The muscles of her abdomen tensed, quivered, waited for the brush of his lips. He didn't disappoint. When his mouth touched the sensitive skin between her legs, she let out a wail of pleasure. She spread her legs to take what he offered, fisting her hands in his hair and tossing her head from side to side. He didn't stop until spasms rocked her body.

* * *

AFTER THEY MADE LOVE, Samirah nestled in his arms, and her eyes drifted closed. He cared deeply for her. She practically floated when she realized it would only be a matter of time before he asked her to stay.

Her impulsive behavior wasn't a mistake this time.

CHAPTER 12

$\mathcal{T}$he trip to the Galapagos Islands excited Samirah. Visiting them had not been part of her original plan, but she was glad to have the opportunity, and even more so to share it with Miguel.

Part of Ecuador, they were a chain of volcanic islands situated over five hundred miles off the coast. In the early 1800s, Charles Darwin had stayed there, and his observations contributed to his theory of evolution and natural selection. Because they were a strictly protected national park, the islands maintained their natural ecosystem. Animals there evolved without natural predators, so they weren't afraid of humans.

At Samirah's suggestion, Miguel offered the Hills the bribe of a small Delgado original sculpture, and they agreed to allow Samirah five days off. Two weeks later, when they got ready to leave for their trip, Geneva was getting around better anyway, using a cane instead of a walker, so Samirah didn't feel any guilt about leaving.

She and Miguel flew from Cuenca to Guayaquil and landed on Baltra Island where they then took a ferry to the first stop, Santa Cruz Island. After half a day of traveling, they took an open-air bus to their seaside lodging. Their small, secluded hotel contained less than fifteen rooms. It was steps away from the beach and within walking distance of the main town.

In the lobby, they met a couple from France celebrating their tenth anniversary with a return to the place where they'd spent their honeymoon.

"How romantic," Samirah said.

"Yes, sometimes he is," the woman, Jeanne, said dryly.

Her husband, Luc, seemed oblivious to her tart reply. "How long will you be on the island?" he asked.

"Three nights," Miguel replied. "On Monday we leave for Isabela. We'll stay there two nights and then we head back to the mainland."

"Oh, but you need at least a week," Jeanne said sorrowfully.

"I have to work, but we plan to make the most of it," Samirah said.

"Come join us on the rooftop terrace later. We're going to have a few drinks before we walk into town for dinner. There is a very good restaurant we remember from our last trip that happens to still be there."

"Sounds like a good idea." Samirah looked at Miguel. "What do you think?"

"Fine with me. We'll meet you later after we spend some time at the beach." They agreed on the time and went their separate ways.

In their room, Samirah and Miguel changed clothes, grabbed their snorkeling gear, and left for Tortuga Bay. They swam and snorkeled the rest of the afternoon on the small beach before making a reluctant return to the hotel.

* * *

LYING on his back on the bed, Miguel watched Samirah fix her hair in the mirror. "What do you call that in English?" he asked. "What you're doing to your hair."

"Cornrows." Her fingers moved quickly as she finished the last of six plaits. She planned to leave her hair in this style for the rest of the trip. He repeated the word to familiarize himself with it. "Not corn-rrrows," she teased. "Cornrows."

He hopped from the bed and grabbed her around the waist. "Are you making fun of my accent?"

She giggled. "Yes."

He nuzzled her neck. "Mmmm. I have to punish you, then."

"*No*. We're already running late for drinks with Jeanne and Luc." Samirah slipped silver hoops into her earlobes.

"How about a...how do you say...quickie?"

She twisted in the circle of his arms and shook her head. Placing her palms against his chest, she said, "Behave yourself," although she could feel the stirrings of her own desire.

He reached under her white tank top at the same time his other hand stroked down the back of her bare leg in a pair of cut off denim shorts. "*Cinco minutos*," he coaxed.

"You always say five minutes, but you always take way longer. Come on." She pushed away his hands. Miguel grumbled in Spanish behind her, but she ignored him and led the way out the door.

They found the French couple seated at a round table on the roof. From the rooftop location, they had a good view of the beach and the road leading into town. The soothing sound of the water and the songs of nature's nocturnal insects blanketed the air.

"There they are!" Luc said. "We thought you had forgotten us."

Samirah smiled. "We spent most of the afternoon snorkeling and enjoyed ourselves so much we lost track of the time."

"I can see you both spent a lot of time in the sun. I am jealous of you. I burn easily."

"We have the rooftop all to ourselves," Jeanne said. She held out two glasses in one hand and a bottle of red wine in the other. "Wine?"

"None for me, thanks," Samirah said.

"I'll have one of those beers," Miguel said, pointing to the small open cooler on the floor of the terrace.

"No problem." Luc handed him a bottle. Miguel sat down and pulled Samirah onto his lap. "So how long have you two been married?"

For the first time since they arrived, Samirah felt uncomfortable. She tensed.

"We're not married," Miguel replied.

"Oh, really? You act like newlyweds. You're an attractive young couple, and from what I can see, you are well-suited to each other." He took a sip of his beer. "Okay, so tell me, what is the relationship here?" Samirah lowered her eyes. She felt Miguel tense and wondered how he would explain their relationship.

"Luc!" his wife said in a mortified voice. She scolded him in colorful French, not knowing Samirah understood every word. "Pardon my husband. I think he has had too much to drink."

"I am not drunk, but please excuse me if I have offended you. Samirah, you're American?"

Samirah nodded. "Next week I'll be back in the States." The thought of going back temporarily saddened her.

"That's too bad." Luc eyed them with interest. "But if you're meant to be together, the distance will be irrelevant."

When neither responded, Jeanne asked if they had plans for dinner. "Why don't you join us?" she added before they could answer. "We will pay for the meal, and we can continue our conversation."

"We couldn't impose."

"You are not imposing," Jeanne said with a dismissive wave of her hand. "Samirah, you'll probably want to change into something else."

"I don't know…" Samirah's eyes found Miguel's to get a cue from him on what he wanted to do.

"Can you not see," Luc drawled in a dry tone, "that my wife is desperate to avoid spending time alone with me? Please, save her." Jeanne's lips tightened and her cheeks colored.

Miguel gave Samirah a reassuring smile. "Sure," he said to the couple.

Samirah rose from his lap to go change and Jeanne got up also. "I will make sure the restaurant can accommodate two more people at our table. We will be back in five minutes."

* * *

Miguel wanted to spend more time alone with Samirah, but knowing her outgoing personality, he assumed she might like to be in the company of other people. He sipped on his beer, his thoughts on the day and what they had planned for tomorrow.

Luc broke the silence between them. "You are a lucky man," he said.

Miguel kept his expression blank. Luc had a sleazy air about him, and he had a feeling he wouldn't like the direction the conversation was about to take.

"I remember my younger days in Paris when I was a single man. The foreign girls who came to visit in the summertime were always so much fun and always looking for a summer romance. It was so easy back then." He sighed. "All I had to do was speak a little French, and soon I had a warm body in my bed."

Miguel thought if he remained quiet, maybe Luc would get the message and shut his mouth before he said something he regretted. No such luck.

"Enjoy your freedom while you can, *amigo*," the man continued. "Once you are married, you will not be able to enjoy beautiful women like Samirah." He lowered his voice to add, "Not out in public, anyway."

Miguel carefully set the beer on the table. The conversation definitely edged in a dangerous direction, and he wanted to put a stop to it. It always happened whenever a gringo called him *amigo*. They assumed their use of the word automatically made them buddies.

"Listen—"

"Between me and you—" Luc glanced over his shoulder at the door, lowering his voice to a conspiratorial level. "I have a mistress, and I think my wife has begun to suspect. It would explain her behavior over the past couple of months. But a man has needs, you know what I mean, *amigo*?"

He was so self-absorbed he remained unaware he carried on a one-sided conversation.

"She is even being difficult on this trip, and it's our anniversary!" Luc sighed dramatically. "Ah, how I envy you! Tonight I will have a cold fish in my bed. While you, my friend..." He laughed knowingly. "You will have that sweet little piece of a—"

Miguel uncoiled his long body from the chair with the speed of a striking rattlesnake. His hand swiped the small table out of the way between them, sending it and the contents—beer, the bottle of wine, and the glasses—crashing to the wooden floor.

Luc stared up at him with his mouth hanging open. Miguel had him on his feet and against the wall with his forearm pressed to his throat before Luc could utter a word. The French man's eyes became wide and terrified in his face.

"Maybe you have no respect for your woman," Miguel said in an even tone, "but you will have respect for mine. She is a goddess. You're not worthy to speak her name."

Only a muddled, gurgling sound could be heard from Luc's throat. Miguel was tempted to crush his windpipe to keep him quiet, but he pulled back. The rage inside him quelled to a quiet hum as he watched Luc lean over the railing to gag and cough to catch his breath.

The last time he experienced such rage had been during a schoolyard fight as a teen. By then he was bigger than most of the boys his age, but one young man hadn't understood the consequences of his words. He didn't tolerate anyone talking about his mother, and he wouldn't tolerate one single inappropriate word about Samirah.

"What is the matter with you?" Luc asked in a strained voice when he finally caught his breath. His eyes were watery and his face still colored a deep red hue. "I paid you a compliment."

Miguel didn't answer, deciding it wasn't worth explaining to the man why his remark was improper. He was certain Luc wouldn't like it if he made such an offhand, inappropriate comment about his wife. He also didn't want to delve any deeper into his violent, visceral reaction.

Seconds after he righted the table, the women returned. They both looked down at the mess on the floor of the terrace with baffled expressions.

"What happened?" Jeanne asked.

"We had a little accident," Luc replied, clutching his throat.

"An accident?" She looked from her husband to Miguel and back again, but neither offered any more details.

To ease the awkwardness of the moment, Miguel moved to stand beside Samirah. "We're on our own for dinner," he said, feigning regret. "It seems Luc has had a change of heart and wants to spend the evening alone with his wife."

Luc cleared his throat. "Yes," he said readily at his wife's confused look.

"How...sweet," Samirah commented, her voice tinged with skepticism. "Maybe we'll see you tomorrow?"

"Maybe." The man cast a wary look in Miguel's direction,

which indicated there was no way in hell he wanted to have anything else to do with them.

After saying their goodbyes, Miguel and Samirah left for the walk into town. Halfway down the stairs to the first floor, Samirah stopped Miguel by placing a hand on his arm. "What really happened back there? It almost looked as if the two of you got into a fight."

"We didn't fight." He took hold of her hand and led the way down the rest of the stairs. "Like Luc said, we had a little accident."

She pursed her lips in disbelief. Rather than give her the opportunity to ask more questions, he placed his arm around her neck and pulled her close as they strolled toward the path to town. "Stop worrying. We're supposed to be having fun, remember?" He gently yanked the end of one of her braids. He didn't want to say anything and have her worry about Luc and his remark.

The corners of her mouth lifted into one of her sweet smiles that made his heart stop. "Okay," she said, putting her arm around his waist. "I'll let you off the hook this time."

A group of four walked ahead of them. The balmy night air whispered across their skin.

"Thank you," he said. He pressed his lips to her temple. "All I want to do is concentrate on eating a good meal and then making love to you for the rest of the night."

"Mmm. Good idea."

She giggled, and the sound caused his chest to tighten, and so did his arm, to draw her closer to him.

* * *

THE REST of the trip was filled with activity. On Saturday, they visited the Charles Darwin Research Station in town and walked the island with a park-certified guide. Samirah snapped photos of the birds and other animals they came across. The guide reminded them not to feed the animals even though they came close, and not to veer off the walking trails. He also cautioned everyone in their small group that when snorkeling, it was fine to swim with the young sea lions because they were very tame, but to stay away from the actual sea lion colonies because the bull lions were dangerous and protective of their turf.

"I'll protect you from the big, bad sea lions," Miguel whispered in her ear.

After Santa Cruz, they traveled to Isabela Island, the largest of the islands in the chain. They spent the next two days there, once again at a small hotel on the beach. On Isabela, Samirah finally got the opportunity to swim with the sea lions, and she saw a blue-footed booby dive down into the water to capture a fish not too far from where she and Miguel snorkeled. She snapped lots of photos, including ones of the giant tortoises, and she let Miguel take a photo of her at the top of the Sierra Negra volcano after their one hour hike.

Late in the afternoon on the last day, they lay on the beach watching the sun go down.

"Do we have to leave tomorrow?" Samirah moaned into his chest.

He wound the end of a braid around his finger. "Unfortunately, yes."

She sighed heavily.

"You enjoyed yourself?" he asked quietly.

"Too much. I wish we could stay longer." She blinked back the tears.

They'd spent every moment together the past five days, and she was spoiled. To go back to their previous routine would be like leaving filet mignon for ground beef. He could barely keep his hands off of her, and their lovemaking was often passionate, and sometimes so sweet and tender it brought tears to her eyes.

"You took a lot of pictures, so you'll have a way to remember this trip."

She raised her head to look into his eyes. "Thank you for bringing me here."

"My pleasure." He brought her face closer to his with his hand at the back of her head. "I'll never forget this time with you."

Why did his words sound so...final?

Samirah licked her lips, forcing a smile to ease the fear pounding through her. "Me either. But we still have the rest of the week to spend together."

Desperate, pathetic. That's how she sounded. Could he see the despair in her eyes?

She kissed his lips, needing to feel close to him right then, needing some reassurance she hadn't made a mistake.

He rose up onto his elbows. "We should go back to the room," he murmured.

"No." She kept him in place with both hands and climbed on top of him.

"Someone might see us." His eyes hazed over in lust as she removed her bikini top.

"Since when do you care about anyone seeing us?" she asked. "No one will see us. The trees are in the way." She didn't care if someone saw them anyway. Acute need and the desire to be close to him twisted through her.

They'd long ago stopped using protection—their passion too wild and spontaneous to be curtailed by its limitations. They made love in the sand, with her on top of him. Her body conformed to his as if it were tailor made to drape across him.

Desperation edged their lovemaking. He filled her with pleasure so sublime she could only cling to him in the aftermath. Tears filled her eyes, and she squeezed them shut to prevent the tears from falling.

He hadn't asked her to stay yet, but she was certain he

would. How could he not, when they'd been so close for weeks and now had spent five wonderful days together? Surely it had been as special for him as it had been for her.

He *would* ask. And she already knew what her answer would be.

She would say yes.

CHAPTER 13

*B*ack in Cuenca, the taxi ride from the airport was a quiet one. Samirah tried not to think about the coming weekend, but it remained at the top of her mind. In just days she would be on a plane back to Miami. Unless the man seated beside her made an offer she couldn't refuse.

She watched him from the corner of her eye. He looked tired, or stressed, or both. Since last night, lines had formed at the corners of his mouth. She wondered if he had similar thoughts to hers. Maybe she should say something—hint she would like to remain in Cuenca for a longer period.

How strange she lacked the nerve to speak her mind, since most of her life she'd never been shy or reserved. But now, when it mattered the most, she couldn't say the words in her heart.

Miguel helped her take her one piece of luggage inside the house when they arrived. After he left, she listened to Geneva gush about her Delgado original and watched her smile and express how lucky Samirah was to be in a relationship with such a talented man.

Funny, she didn't feel lucky at the moment.

She spent the rest of the day catching up on her household duties. She also went into town to purchase items at the market and took the opportunity to mail the souvenirs she'd purchased while in the Galapagos.

She didn't eat much at dinner. Both Geneva and Thomas expressed their concern, but she assured them she wasn't sick, just tired.

She wouldn't be able to see Miguel again until the next day when Geneva went to her therapy appointment. Tomorrow was Thursday, which meant only two more days before her departure. Surely he would say something then.

* * *

THE FOLLOWING DAY, to keep her mind off her melancholy thoughts, Samirah pulled out her notebook with her restaurant ideas and flipped through the pages, reviewing the sketches, color schemes, and the sample menus. She did some doodling but didn't accomplish much because her thoughts ran constantly to Miguel.

When she heard her employers call out a goodbye on their way to the appointment, she slammed the notebook closed and hopped off the bed. The taxi disappeared from sight before she slipped on a pair of sandals and went over to Miguel's. She'd made up her mind she would bring up the topic of her staying.

Why should she be afraid to mention it? She loved him, and even if he didn't love her, she knew he cared about her. He enjoyed her company and had taken her on a lovely trip where they'd spent their days and nights like a couple in love.

"There's nothing to fear but fear itself," she whispered as she entered Miguel's house. He always kept the door open for her on the days she came over so she could come in while he worked in the studio. Except he wasn't in the studio today.

Frowning, she made her way upstairs to his bedroom. Once

there, the sight that greeted her eyes made her heart jump. A suitcase was opened on his bed, and he stood over an open dresser drawer, removing clothes.

"What's going on?"

He straightened suddenly, surprised to see her, even though she always came by around this time.

The tension lines around his mouth were even more pronounced than the day before. "Aarón called," he said by way of explanation. "I have to go."

Miguel loved his younger brother and wanted to protect him, but she didn't quite understand what from. It had to do with his own past and his strained relationship with his mother, but she'd never fully understood the gist of it, and he never seemed to want to confide in her.

"What's wrong? Has something happened to him?"

His fingers brushed the hair back from his face. The muscles of his arm flexed with the movement, but she remained focused on the man and what seemed to be a difficult time for him.

He rested the edge of his butt against the dresser. "My mother has decided to take him with her to Germany, even though she promised we would discuss it. Aarón wants to come live with me. He doesn't want to be dragged to Europe to yet another house with another man who..." He expelled a heavy breath. "Who doesn't really want him around anyway."

Samirah's gaze landed on the open suitcase again. "When do you leave?"

"Tonight. I'm catching the next flight out to Miami."

A feeling of dread crept over her. "Were you going to tell me?"

"Of course. I had no intention of leaving without saying goodbye. I wanted to get my things together first because there isn't much time if I want to catch the flight."

She nodded her understanding, even though the word "goodbye" held a finality that couldn't be missed. "Do you need me to do anything while you're gone? Stock the fridge with groceries, get his room ready?"

"No." He raked his fingers through his hair again and stared at the suitcase instead of her.

"You sure?" Her voice sounded the way she felt—small and insignificant. Because she understood what was taking place, and she didn't want to face it. When he didn't reply, she asked, "How long will you be gone?"

"I hope only a few days, but it could be longer."

This was it. The dump. He no longer needed her.

"Should—should I—"

"Samirah."

Her teeth sank into the tender flesh of the inside of her bottom lip. Over the past twenty-four hours, she'd agonized over what would happen and how she would feel if he didn't ask her to stay as she'd hoped he would, but nothing could prepare her for the excruciating pain she experienced at this moment.

"This isn't how I wanted things to go," he said. "I wanted us to spend as much time together as possible over these next couple of days, but—but these are circumstances out of my control. I want you to know I've enjoyed every moment we've spent together. It was fun."

Her eyes snapped up to his. "Fun? I've been *fun*? Is that supposed to be some kind of compliment?"

He looked exasperated. "Don't do this."

"Don't do what? Tell you the truth about yourself?"

"Don't make this into something ugly."

"Don't worry, Miguel. You've already done a really good job of that on your own."

He pushed off the dresser. "What do you want me to say?"

"I thought you…cared about me. I came here to tell you…"

The pain of rejection clogged her throat, and her voice kept breaking. She couldn't stand the look of pity in his eyes so she stared down at the carpet, finding it hard to believe it would end this way. She covered her face with her hands so she could hide behind them. She was falling apart. For the first time in her life, she wanted to hide and didn't want to be seen.

He came silently over to her and grasped her wrists. "Samirah, *querida.*"

"Stop," she whispered. "I told you not to call me that."

"I've been calling you that for a long time now."

"But you don't mean it."

"Of course I mean it. Look at me." She allowed him to lower her hands, and he tilted up her face with a finger under her chin. "We both knew from the beginning our time together would be short. You have your life in Miami, and your family in the States. I knew you would be leaving. So instead of saying our goodbyes on Saturday, we're saying them a couple of days early. It has always been inevitable."

For you, but not for me.

Her throat seized up. She should have known it wouldn't last, but she'd gotten caught up in the dream, and now reality had taken hold. The pain of her last sordid relationship paled in comparison to the gutting she experienced now.

How could he truly care about her if he was willing to walk away so easily?

"So you care, you just don't care enough to see where this relationship can go?" Was that her voice, sounding so raw and thick with hopelessness?

"This is exciting to you now, but in a few months you'll be bored and ready to move on."

"Don't tell me what I think and what I feel!"

"I don't have to, you already said it!" He became very still, the bones in his face sharpening in direct proportion to the tension mounting in the room. "'Why would you want to stay in the same place when you can go anywhere you want?'"

Samirah stepped back. "You're using my words against me."

"I'm not using them against you. I'm simply repeating what you said."

"That's not fair," she said with a vigorous shake of her head.

"And then there's always your restaurant on South Beach, 'where all the action is.'"

Her brow line creased. "Why are you doing this?"

"Because you want something that's unrealistic," he replied in a fierce voice. "You would never be happy here. You could never be happy in a place where the most excitement that takes place is our national holidays and a fundraiser for the arts. You expect me to believe you could live like this, in a modest house in a quiet neighborhood?"

"You don't even know me. Yes, I said those things, but that's not what I meant."

"How else could you mean it? Why would you say those things and not mean them?"

"The conversation took place weeks ago. I've been in this neighborhood for over two months and I do love it."

"For now," he said. "Relationships take work."

"I know."

"You have to start out on some kind of compatible foundation. What do we have? Great sex and a trip to the Galapagos?"

The blunt words jarred her. "That's all it was to you?"

Pain blossomed in her body. She could feel it everywhere—in her eyes, in her heart, in her soul. Was that all she was good for? A roll in the hay? A screw, an affair, and then on to the next woman? This relationship was much more than a mere fling to her.

"Dammit, Samirah. This wasn't supposed to be—"

"No!" She covered his mouth with her hand. "Don't say it."

She knew how the sentence ended. This wasn't supposed to be...serious, long term, permanent, forever, a real relationship.

She removed her hand and stepped back, frightened by the fact that despite everything he said, she still wanted him. His touch blistered her skin, the softness of his mouth against her palm made her tingle and want to feel those same lips against hers again.

"You're right." In her fight for control, she spoke in a cool voice. "I don't want to stay here. Why would I? Like you said, what's in Cuenca? I mean, it's not even Quito, or Guayaquil. It's too slow for me, and I need excitement and *fun*."

His stance became rigid. Not one single muscle on his body moved except the one flexing in his left jaw. "Which is what I said."

"You were right."

"So it's over." His blue gaze lowered to her mouth. "How about a goodbye kiss?"

She laughed. "You must be kidding." She turned swiftly, but his words halted her at the door.

"I told you never to walk away from me again."

She stared at him. "Our conversation is finished."

"No, it's not."

"You get to dictate the terms of our relationship *and* when it ends, *and* you get to tell me when our conversation is over? My, my, aren't you the man in charge."

"I've warned you about your mouth. It will always get you into trouble unless you learn to keep it shut."

"I guess I'll always be in trouble."

She stormed out of the room. A third of the way down the stairs, Miguel's muscular arms wound around her waist and pulled her into his chest. She began to struggle with him, pushing and pulling.

"Stop it or you'll make us fall down the stairs." When she stilled her movements, he spoke into her ear. "Kiss me." She shook her head wildly, determined to refuse his request.

Strong fingers grasped her chin and held her head in place. He pressed her back against the wall. "Kiss me," he repeated, staring into her eyes. "Please."

Samirah's heart filled with sadness. This was the man she loved, and it was the last time she would see him.

The lines of her lips softened, and Miguel settled his mouth over hers. Burying his fingers in her hair, he held her head in place so he could give one of the sweetest kisses he'd ever offered to her. Their mouths glided over one another, tender, soft. He tasted good, smelled good. Her heart ached at the unfairness of it.

He pressed closer so the tips of her breasts grazed his chest. A throbbing ache blossomed at the apex of her thighs. She wanted him, one last time. Her fingers splayed across his back, drawing him closer, curling into the muscles. She lifted onto her toes, aching, needing…

Miguel withdrew, and Samirah reluctantly dropped her hands to her sides. Her humiliation was complete. While he had the strength to pull away, she'd been ready to let him make love to her.

"Will you let me go now?" She swallowed the pain and stared at the ridges and curves of his bare chest. "It's over. Let's just make a clean break."

He remained silent, but she saw the fingers of left hand ball up into a fist at his side. She slipped away from him and he didn't stop her. She wished he would, but of course, he didn't.

At the house, she slid under the covers in her bedroom.

Fool. *Fool.* She closed her eyes.

Cast aside again. Only this time, it was much worse. Before, she'd been embarrassed and hurt by the failed relationship with her boss. This time, the gut-wrenching pain threatened to rend her in two.

She pressed her face into the pillow and curled into a ball. No tears came.

She just lay there.

Numb.

* * *

MIGUEL HURRIEDLY SHOVED clothes into his suitcase.

He wanted to possess her. Lock her up and toss the key so she could never escape. Instead, he'd let her go.

He'd done the right thing. She would never be happy in this sedate existence. She was too full of life and energy and would grow to resent him if she stayed. To ask her to stay would be beyond selfish.

The blare of the taxi's horn accelerated his movements. He snapped the suitcase closed and scanned the room to make sure he hadn't missed anything. His eyes settled on the jar of lotion on the dresser, and he lifted the container to his nose and sniffed.

This was Samirah's scent. His gut tightened like a knotted rope. He'd wanted her one last time, and she had been willing, malleable in his arms. But it would have been unfair to her, so he'd forced himself to pull back.

I did the right thing, he told himself again.

Even though he'd seen the pain in her brown eyes, he knew this was the best decision for both of them. If he allowed her to stay any longer, she would only become more entrenched in his life, and then he would never be able to let her go when she got ready to leave. Because without a doubt, there would come a time when she would want to leave.

He replaced the jar on top of the furniture.

He'd known it couldn't last, but that didn't lessen the pain. He would miss her—her laugh, her awful singing, and her incredible, giving body he couldn't imagine ever getting enough of.

The horn sounded again, and Miguel grabbed his suitcase. He couldn't miss this flight. His brother needed him. Aarón had finally confided in him about the verbal abuse from his mother's lover. He was petrified of going abroad, and talking to their mother did no good. She refused to believe a man so cultured could be so cruel and assumed Aarón must have done something or was exaggerating.

Miguel knew it to be true, though he'd never witnessed any of the abuse. He'd experienced the same himself as a child, and only when he reached puberty and grew taller did the men become less confrontational.

He rushed down the stairs, but his hurried footsteps stalled at the front door. A vase of flowers sat on a table. Pictures Samirah had purchased hung on the wall, bringing color and life to his formerly pallid existence.

He'd made the right decision.

Miguel yanked open the front door and slammed it hard. Ecuador would become a distant memory when she went off to her next adventure. She would forget all about him.

And he would have to figure out how to forget about her.

* * *

As the end of her trip grew closer, Samirah did a poor job of hiding her sadness. Geneva and Thomas expressed their concern, telling her she could come back and visit any time she liked. They thought she was upset about leaving the country, but it was so much more complicated than they knew.

On Saturday morning, they escorted her to the waiting taxi. Geneva still walked with the cane, but she was much more mobile than when Samirah first arrived.

"Thank you so much, my dear. You were absolutely lovely." Geneva kissed each of her cheeks.

Thomas gave her a big hug. "Have a safe trip back."

"I enjoyed my stay. I couldn't have asked for better employers."

Impulsively, she gave them each another quick hug before jumping into the cab. As it pulled away, she waved through the back window. Thomas stood with his arm around his wife, and they both waved at her until the cab turned the corner.

Samirah took a deep breath, telling herself she would be fine. She had her future to plan, but living in Miami didn't have the same appeal, and neither did heading off to another job overseas. Not with her heart firmly anchored in this little South American country she'd never expected to fall in love with. Not when she realized loving Miguel might have been the best and worst mistake she ever made.

She rummaged in her carry-on bag and found the cell phone she used for emergencies. Her fingers trembled as she dialed her sister's number in Los Angeles.

"Hello?"

"Bekah, it's me."

"Hey, Samirah! I guess you're at the airport getting ready to catch your flight, huh?"

The sound of her sister's cheerful voice broke her. She'd made it through the past couple of days without crying. But now, tears spilled onto her cheeks and she wiped them away, only to have them replaced by new ones.

Rebekah's alarmed voice came over the line. "Honey, what's wrong?"

"Bekah, I really screwed up this time. Can I come see you? *Please.*"

CHAPTER 14

*O*n the opulent kitchen of her German lover's home, Patricia Delgado stood at the marble island and dipped her fork into a bowl full of sliced fruit. She wore tight clothes—a pair of skintight black slacks and a white, ruffled blouse with the top buttons undone to expose her surgically enhanced cleavage. Every type of jewel glittered on her fingers, around her neck and wrists, and in her ears. The effects of Botox kept her face free of the lines typical of someone her age, and she had the body of a much younger woman, thanks to the best plastic surgery money could buy.

The bright colors of the peaches, mangos, and pineapples in the bowl reminded Miguel of Samirah. Everything reminded him of her. Sunshine, beaches, motorcycles, food. Everything. He couldn't stop thinking about her, knowing they stayed in the same city, and he had no way of getting in touch.

"I love him, you know," Patricia said.

Miguel struggled to remember what they had been talking about before his mind drifted to thoughts of Samirah. "Yes, I know."

"He loves me, too. It's different this time."

It was always different "this time." It had been different when she left him at the age of fifteen to fend for himself as she moved with her Colombian lover. It had been different with the Mexican, the Swede, the Canadian, the Englishman—he'd lost count of the men over the years. The only common denominator between them all was their wealth.

"I know," he said again, though he didn't believe a word of it. In another year or so, she would be replaced by another woman, perhaps someone younger, and then she would take whatever parting gifts the German gave her until she could find another sponsor.

Love was never a factor in the relationships between his mother and her lovers. All her relationships ended the same way, except for the one she had with Aarón's father, a seventy-five-year-old man who married her when she became pregnant. He imagined his mother had expected that upon his death she would be left with a vast fortune.

Unfortunately, the old man had been keeping secrets. When he died, his so-called wealth disappeared in back taxes and risky deals gone awry. He'd barely been staying afloat. The small settlement she received had been negligible, and she'd had to sell her jewelry and other gifts to maintain the type of lifestyle to which she'd become accustomed.

Miguel had spent the last few days trying to convince his mother to let him have Aarón, yet she refused to give a definitive answer. He even pointed out how much easier her life would be if she didn't have a child to worry about. The argument seemed to sway her somewhat, but still, she would not say yes.

Patricia spoke again. "I know what you think of me."

His mouth set in a grim line. He was in no mood for theatrics. They needed to come to an agreed upon decision about Aarón.

"Mother—"

"I know, Miguel. I see it. You don't have to deny it, because I *know*." She picked up the bowl of fruit.

Her stilettos clicked on the tile on her way to the sink. She always wore heels. He couldn't remember the last time he'd seen her with anything else on her feet. Resting her hands on the sink, she said, "He's my son."

He stared at the back of her head and the neat ponytail of midnight-colored hair. "He wants you, not your son. I can take care of Aarón, protect him."

"There is nothing to protect him from."

"You don't believe that. You know the truth, even if you refuse to accept it. He's your son. Doesn't he deserve better?"

She spun around, her eyes flashing angrily. "I can give him everything his heart desires. Look at all of this. Can you give him this, Miguel?"

"No, but I can give him love, and I can give him stability. I can give you the same, but what I have to offer is not good enough for you."

He may not be as rich as this man, but he was wealthy in his own right. He could afford to live in more lavish surroundings, but he chose to live modestly because of how he'd grown up. He lived below his means, never wanting to be so desperate for money and status he'd do anything for it. Like his mother.

Patricia swallowed, and her eyes filled with tears. He could see the struggle within her, and he knew the answer he wanted was soon forthcoming.

"You always had so much rage inside of you, so much anger at the world—always fighting."

She had no idea it was all because of her, or she pretended not to. It was so hard to tell. Frustration at his situation and anger because of the things children said about her had fueled that rage, and he'd felt compelled to defend her honor, even though he understood what she did. She was still his mother.

"I know you think I became pregnant on purpose, but I didn't. It's true I expected more after his father died, but…I didn't want Aarón at first. Then I thought it might be a way for me to do everything over, since I'd failed you. Maybe this time I could…I don't know…redeem myself. Prove to you and everyone else I'm more than just a rich man's whore."

Her words triggered something in Miguel. Samirah. Had he treated her as such, ending the relationship even though he knew she had feelings for him and he for her? He accepted he had fallen in love with her, despite his best efforts to keep the relationship casual. Being in Miami under the current circumstances was bad enough, but missing Samirah made it one hundred times more difficult.

He'd been afraid he'd lose Samirah the same way he'd lost his mother all those years ago, but Samirah was nothing like her. Samirah had a kind and generous heart. She made everyone smile. She played with the neighborhood children and helped people with their English. Money, the single most important thing in his mother's life—more important than her own children—didn't matter to Samirah. She told him herself she would travel to other countries and stay until the money ran out.

What had he done?

He gripped the counter as a trembling shook his entire body. He'd sent her away and now he had no idea how to get in touch with her. He had to find her and tell her he'd made a terrible mistake.

"Miguel, are you listening to me?" He resurfaced into the present. "What's wrong with you? You look pale. You've been acting strangely ever since you arrived."

"Nothing. What did you say?"

Sadness crossed his mother's features. "I said I won't force Aarón to come with me to Germany. You can take him back to Ecuador with you."

* * *

Samirah walked into the kitchen to find her sister at the stove pouring coconut milk into a pot of Caribbean pelau, a dish their mother had taught them to make at a young age. It was Monday afternoon. After hearing her oldest nephew ask in the hallway outside the bedroom if Aunt Samirah was sick, she realized she was not being a good guest and should stop wallowing in self-pity by hiding out in the spare bedroom.

Rebekah looked up from stirring the pot. "Hi hon, how are you feeling?"

Samirah shrugged. "I've been better."

Her sister covered the pot and smiled sympathetically at her. There were only three years between them, but Rebekah had always been so much more mature and responsible. Except when she eloped with Rafael Lopez at the age of eighteen. How she'd envied her sister her freedom and escape from being under their father's strict rule. But then Rebekah had moved back home after her marriage fell apart, and almost ten years passed before she and Rafael reconciled.

"You know, I just realized you owe me," Samirah said to lighten the mood.

"Oh, really?" Rebekah placed one hand on her hip, wider now because she was almost eight months pregnant with her fourth child. Outside, Samirah could see her brother-in-law, Rafael, her twelve-year-old nephew, and the two-year-old twins in the pool.

"Yep. Considering after you eloped, Dad turned into a prison warden who monitored my every move and made my life a living hell."

She picked a piece of lettuce from the bowl of salad her sister had prepared and munched on it.

"Yeah, sorry about that. But you do realize if I'd never run off, you wouldn't have had an incentive to leave home and see the world. You should be thanking me."

"Really? That's what you're going with?"

Rebekah nodded and they both laughed.

"Have you decided to find out what you're having yet?" Samirah asked. She was avoiding the inevitable conversation. "You look like you're carrying twins again."

Her sister had said she was tired of all the testosterone in the house and wanted a girl, but she refused to find out if she carried a girl or a boy.

"Thanks, but I'm not," Rebekah said dryly. "I'm a little offended by your remark. I'm not that big."

"Mhmm. You guys are going to need a bigger place soon. You're already almost out of space with all these kids."

"Why does everybody keep saying 'all these kids'? I have three. Only three."

"It seems like a lot, though. Maybe because they're all boys and they're always so loud. Huh. Yeah, you only have three."

"Well, four, if you count their father," Rebekah said.

A faint smile came to her lips as she watched her husband roar and jump into the water. The two youngest yelled and clapped excitedly, their little legs kicking frantically as they swam toward him with the floatation devices around their waists. Meanwhile, Ricardo, the oldest boy, came up from behind and jumped on his father's back.

"I'm still hoping it's a girl, but according to him—" She lowered her voice and affected a Spanish accent. "Lopez men only make boys."

Samirah grinned at her sister's imitation of her husband's voice. "He might be right. There are a lot of men in his family."

Rebekah heaved a sigh. "I know. But I'm not giving up hope." She rubbed her belly and gave Samirah a questioning look. "Are you ready to talk about it?"

"Sure. You start. Go ahead. Say it."

"Say what?"

"I told you so."

"I wasn't going to say I told you so." Her sister's eyes filled with sympathy.

"Don't. I don't want you to feel sorry for me. You should be chewing me out, considering we had a deal I wouldn't get involved with anyone while in Ecuador. I was supposed to be taking a break and getting my head together. I need you to yell at me and make me feel bad."

"What for? I'm sure you already feel bad enough as it is."

Just then, Rafael entered the kitchen. He had a towel slung around his neck, which he'd obviously used to pat himself dry before coming into the house. "Samirah, you're alive. I was beginning to doubt you were really here."

"Don't tease her, she's not feeling well."

"I'm fine. Don't listen to her."

Rafael shrugged, as if he didn't understand the strange conversations of women. "How long before dinner's ready?" he asked. He moved to stand beside Rebekah. He towered over her, a big, beefy man who didn't seem to have lost much of the muscle he had packed on before he retired from professional wrestling years ago.

"Thirty-five to forty minutes."

"Okay, I'll get the boys out of the pool." He bent his head to her belly. "Hello *mijo*, how are you doing? Dinner is soon served."

"Rafe, stop, it's a girl. Say *my daughter*."

He chuckled, a very masculine laugh. "She's so cute when she's in denial, isn't she?" he said to Samirah. "If it's a boy, we'll keep trying until you get your girl, okay, *mi amor*?" He dropped a light kiss on her mouth and then pinched her bottom.

"Rafe!"

He chuckled again on his way back out the door and called for the boys to get out of the pool.

"Make sure they dry off before coming inside," Rebekah yelled after him. She took Samirah by the arm. "Come on, let's go in the living room where we can talk. In a minute you're about to hear something like the sound of stampeding buffalo running through the house."

They sat on the sofa and Samirah told her sister the entire story, from the time she met Miguel to the day they said goodbye.

At one point, Rebekah interrupted her. "On top of a car in the middle of a parking lot outside of a fundraiser? Weren't you worried you'd get caught?"

"It crossed my mind, but it wasn't my biggest concern at the time."

"Apparently not. Continue."

At the end, Samirah heaved a heavy sigh. "Being with Miguel was the first time since I left Mom and Dad's that I felt I had a home. Don't get me wrong, I've had a lot of fun traveling around the world, but with him, I got so comfortable. It felt good. It felt right."

"I don't think you could've done anything different, hon. You have to give it time."

Samirah looked into her sister's eyes. "Does the pain ever go away?"

Rebekah pursed her lips. "You know how it was after Rafe and I broke up. I have to be honest, it never goes away." She took Samirah's hand. "But it does get easier."

"I wish he'd asked me to stay," Samirah whispered brokenly. "I would have stayed, Bekah. If he'd asked me to."

* * *

LATER IN THE EVENING, they were all in the media room watching a movie on the pull-down screen. The twins and Ricardo sprawled on the floor with bowls of popcorn. Rebekah sat curled into Rafael's body on one end of the sofa, with his hand resting protectively on her stomach. Samirah sat on the other end of the sofa with her feet under her.

The phone rang and Rafael reached for it on the side table. Looking at the Caller I.D., he said, "It's your brother."

"Hey, Adam," Samirah heard her sister say.

She returned her eyes to the screen. The movie was something about a family and talking zoo animals. She stifled a yawn.

"Adam, wait a minute, calm down. She's right here." Rebekah sat up from Rafael and her gaze met Samirah's. "Wait, what did you say? Miguel?"

Samirah's heart leapt in her chest. She crawled across the sofa and pressed her ear to the phone so she could hear.

"I don't know who the hell this Miguel guy is," Adam was saying, "but he insists he knows Sam. The clients she worked for in Ecuador gave him the name and address of my firm. He came into my offices and scared the hell out of my secretary while I was out to lunch, demanding to know Sam's whereabouts. Then he came back again this afternoon, and we got into a shouting match. What did she do down there? She was supposed to be working."

"She was working."

Samirah took the phone. Her palms were so sweaty she thought it might slip from her fingers. "Adam, what exactly did he say?" she asked breathlessly.

She rose from the sofa and helped her sister up.

"Sam, is that you? What's going on? Is this guy bothering you? Do I need to get a couple of my frat brothers together to have a talk with him?"

They hurried into the living room and Rebekah picked up the extension in there.

"No, Adam, no. Tell me what he said."

"He said he's coming back tomorrow, that's what he said. This is the first chance I've had to call you, but I can tell you, I'm still pretty pissed by this Miguel guy. He acts as if he owns you or something. Damn, Sam, can't you stay out of trouble for two minutes? What happened down there? You were supposed to be working."

"I did work, Adam. I made your clients very happy."

"Darn it, Adam, tell her the rest of it!"

"Calm down, pregnant lady." Rebekah rolled her eyes and Samirah bit back a laugh. "He started talking about how much he loves you and he made a mistake letting you go and he needed to know where he could find you. I tried to explain to him we can't divulge employee personal information, but he wouldn't listen. He said he's coming back tomorrow and some-body's going to tell him where you are because he's not leaving Miami without you. I didn't like those comments. What's he planning to do, kidnap you?"

"He said that?" Samirah whispered, clutching the phone. "He said he wouldn't leave without me?"

"Yes, those are his words. What the hell did you do to this guy—or do I need to ask?"

"He said he loves me?" Samirah said in the same soft voice. She looked across the room at her sister.

A few seconds of silence before her brother replied. "Yeah, he said he loves you." Quiet again. "Sam, what do you want me to do?"

She was shaking. "Adam, let me call you back, okay?"

"All right. I'll be up for awhile."

Samirah set the phone on the table. She couldn't move on her shaky legs. "Bekah?" She didn't know what she was asking. She'd wanted to hear those words, but she was so afraid to reach for what he offered.

Rebekah rushed across the room and clasped her sister's

hands between her own. "Do you remember what you told me when I said Rafe and I were going to try to work things out?" Samirah shook her head. At the moment, she could barely remember the day of the week. "You said I should do what makes me happy. So I'm giving you the same advice. If the two of you love each other, don't waste a lot of years apart like Rafe and I did. Do what makes you happy."

$\mathcal{M}$iguel stood on the crowded sidewalk outside the restaurant where he and Samirah had agreed to meet two days ago. South Beach night life was full of pedestrian traffic and cars crept along, creating a traffic jam as their drivers showed off their shiny rides and watched the passersby.

Only seven days had passed since he last saw her, but it felt like an eternity. He couldn't wait. But how did she feel? She hadn't revealed much when they talked on the phone, and nervous energy coursed through him. Their brief phone conversation had been used only to inform him that the man he'd yelled at in the placement agency was her brother and to set up this meeting. He worried that even though she agreed to see him, she still might not forgive him.

He swallowed down the fear. There was never a time in his life when he wanted anything so much. Before her, he'd simply been existing, but with her, he'd started to live. She'd brought color and excitement into his world, and there was no way he could go back to Ecuador without her.

From a distance he saw her cross the street before she saw him, dressed in two tank tops layered over each other and a long skirt that billowed around her ankles. With so many people milling about, she appeared then disappeared in between them. She must have done her hair in cornrows again and let it out because it flowed down her back in the same wavy pattern as the last day he'd seen her. Large gold hoops dangled in her ears and her wrists were filled with bangles.

Too impatient to wait for her approach, he moved toward her, irritated as several men turned around on the sidewalk to look at her. When she saw him, her steps slowed and came to a complete halt. He kept moving, in between people ambling close together and talking. Past the crowded restaurant tables set up on the sidewalk café-style.

Finally, when he stood before her, he stared at her lovely face and thought about what a fool he'd been to ever let her go. He'd wanted to fly out to Los Angeles to see her right away, but she'd told him she would come to Miami in a couple of days. He'd waited—two days, nine hours, and fifty-seven minutes to see her.

"Hi," she said, looking vaguely uncomfortable under his intense stare.

He let his eyes travel down the length of her body. Her beautiful breasts sat high on her chest, and the tank tops hugged her curves in such a way he wanted to smooth his hands along the womanly lines. She looked like a goddess with her wild, wavy hair and colorful clothes.

"How are you?" he asked.

"Fine."

"You look…exquisite."

"Thank you." She said the words almost shyly. So unlike her. "How are you?"

A strange conversation for two people who knew each other as intimately as they did. "Not good. I missed you."

"You mentioned that over the phone already." He tried not to let the dismissal of his words bother him. He would willingly accept whatever punishment she meted out as long as she agreed to go back with him. "How's Aarón?"

"He's with my mother. He's coming back to Ecuador with us."

One eyebrow arched upward. "You're being rather presumptuous, aren't you? I didn't say I would go back with you."

"You don't have to. I already know you will because I'm not giving you a choice. Don't say a word," he added when her mouth opened to no doubt laser him with a smart aleck retort. "Let's go to the other side where it's quieter."

Without waiting for an answer, he weaved his fingers through hers, and she didn't pull away. As they waited for a lull in the traffic to cross the street, he brought the back of her hand to his lips, closed his eyes, and inhaled the fragrant scent of her skin.

When he opened his eyes, the look in hers cut him to the core. The depth of the pain he'd caused her was there for him to see, and her lip quivered before she turned her face away.

He cursed himself for what he'd done. He would do anything to make it up to her.

The beach side of the street was dimmer without the barrage of lights from hotels and restaurants running along it. The ocean roared on the other side of the trees and greenery separating it from where they stood.

"Miguel, you're squeezing my hand too tight."

He loosened his hold, but didn't—couldn't let her go. "I don't know where to begin."

Those same soul-filled eyes looked up at him, and all he wanted to do was draw her close and promise never to hurt her again.

"I don't understand what happened," she said. "You told Adam you love me, but if you do, why didn't you tell me, and why did you let me go?"

He shook his head at the foolishness of his decision, which

had seemed so sound at the time. His lightly calloused thumb stroked across the soft skin of her hand. "Because I was a fool. I let you go because I thought you would never be happy in a little city in a little country in South America. All I could think about was all the places you'd visited and I wondered why would you want to stay there with me." His face tightened as he readied himself to share a piece of his past. "The truth is, I lost someone before, and I didn't want it to happen again. I was trying to protect myself—my pride, my feelings—because you came to mean more to me than I ever imagined you would."

He then recounted the story of his mother's departure for Colombia. He also told her about the first woman he fell in love with as a young man. The love he felt then couldn't compare to the feelings he had for Samirah now, but at the time, the loss had been brutal.

Those episodes in his life helped to form his future relationships, keeping them for the most part casual without certainty or promises for the future. In that way, he would never have to feel the pain of separation again.

SAMIRAH LISTENED WITH SYMPATHETIC EARS, wondering how any woman could leave her son to follow after a man. She realized how fortunate she was to be close to her siblings and have been raised by two loving parents, even if they were overbearing— especially her father. His love for his children caused him to be overprotective, and no matter how much she resented it growing up, the alternative looked even less appealing.

"I thought maybe my feelings were one-sided," she said. "I wondered if our relationship was only about sex for you. Less than a year ago, I was in a relationship that ended badly. He lied to me and used me. It was just about sex for him, and I wondered if it was the same for you. Maybe you didn't feel the same way and...maybe you didn't even respect me."

"How could you think I didn't respect you?" A sharp frown creased his face and made him look angry. "I almost put a man through a wall for you!"

Samirah stared at him in shock. "What are you talking about?"

"Never mind, I'll explain later." He took a few moments to gather his thoughts. "I do love you. Because I do, I can't go back without you. Did your brother tell you I said that, too? My life hasn't been the same since you entered it. I didn't know what I was missing, and now that I do, I can't live like I did before." His fingers tightened around hers. "It won't be the same, though. My brother will be living with me. No more skinny dipping in the middle of the night or walking around the house naked." He hoped to elicit a smile, and he did.

"Are you going to be okay with that?" Samirah asked.

"I'll learn to live without it." A smile hovered around his lips.

He said he loved her, but he didn't make any promises beyond that. Samirah closed her eyes. Dare she take the risk?

"Samirah?" She could hear the heavy weight of worry in his voice.

Do what makes you happy.

She opened her eyes. "I'm certain I want to be with you, but are you sure? You really hurt me."

"I know. Let me fix it. Let me make it up to you. There was never a doubt in my mind that I wanted to be with you. It's because I wanted you so much that I thought it best to cut off our relationship. I thought it would be too hard later when you decided to leave." He swallowed. "I know I hurt you, and maybe you hate me a little bit because of it, but I need you in my life." He paused, and the earnest expression in his face tipped the balance in his favor. "Hate me in Cuenca."

"I don't know how to hate you," Samirah said softly. "So I

guess I'll have to love you in Cuenca." A slow smile spread across her face.

"I like your idea better." He smiled back. *"Ven aquí, querida,"* he said, pulling her into his arms.

They held onto each other for a little while before she smirked up at him. "I can't make this too easy for you, so I have one condition to coming back."

"You want to hang me up by my toenails? Submit me to Chinese water torture?"

"No. If I come back, no more comments about my singing. I'm singing every day, and you can't complain."

"Uh, what about options one and two?"

"Miguel!" She punched him softly, her fist hitting nothing but rock hard abs. "It's a joke."

"I know, *querida.*" He lowered his head and tasted her lips, kissing her softly. "I'm joking too. I love your singing."

"Mentiroso," she whispered.

He laughed, and his warm breath brushed across her lips. "It's a little lie," he admitted. Suddenly, his expression sobered and he cupped her face in his big hands. "But I'm telling you the truth when I tell you I love you. Do you believe me?"

She nodded. She took the softness of his kiss and burrowed her face in his chest, taking a deep breath to revel in his clean male scent. "Has it only been a week?"

"I know, it feels so much longer." He kissed the corner of her mouth, her cheek, and trailed even more kisses down her neck. Her body awoke under the tender caresses of his lips. "It's been too long since I've licked you." His tongue slid along the sensitive spot behind her ear. A delicious shiver ran down her spine. "Kissed you." He pressed his mouth against hers. "Tasted you." His tongue dipped between her lips, and she moaned, softening against him.

"Where do you stay?" he asked, his hands roaming impatiently across her back.

"Within walking distance in a ridiculously overpriced apartment," she answered, popping the top button on his shirt to plant a kiss on his chest below his corded necklace.

"Good. Lead the way."

They stood pressed against each other and enjoyed a long kiss before they hurried down the sidewalk in the direction of her apartment.

CHAPTER 16

"*A*arón!" Samirah called up the stairs. "Hurry up or you'll miss the bus." She made her way back into the kitchen and the breakfast she'd prepared that he wouldn't have time to eat.

She shook her head when she heard him come bounding down the stairs. He rushed into the kitchen with his book bag on his back, his face flushed and worried.

"You're really pushing it, mister. You know you'll be in big trouble with Miguel if you miss it again."

"Sorry, Samirah."

"Don't be sorry. Just hurry up."

Aarón shoved a few forkfuls of scrambled eggs into his mouth and grabbed a piece of toast. Samirah handed him his lunch money and he raced toward the door. She followed and stood in the doorway to watch him, but he stopped at the bottom of the steps and came rushing back to the door.

"What did you forget?"

"Nothing." He hesitated for a minute, and then he gave her a hug, holding onto her with surprising strength, crushing her arms to her sides so she couldn't reciprocate. "Thanks," he mumbled, a soft tremor in his voice.

Then he dashed off, and one of his new friends from another house joined him in the race up the street. She hoped he didn't miss the bus. Last time Miguel had grounded him for a week because he had to take him to school on his motorcycle. No hanging out with friends in the neighborhood, no video games, and no television.

Poor kid. She could tell he'd been through a lot. After six weeks, Miguel was still working on him, but they'd gotten closer, and even though Aarón pouted whenever he received a punishment for some infraction, he obviously needed the structure.

He certainly brought out her maternal instincts and made her think about having kids of her own. Although she and Miguel had talked about the possibility of marriage, they hadn't made any final decisions yet.

If their relationship progressed to that point, she only wanted one or two. Not four, like her sister. The video clip Rebekah and Rafael sent a few weeks ago showed a healthy baby boy. Rafael's smug face had declared to the camera, "I guess we'll have to keep trying."

She closed the door and went into Miguel's studio. A large sculpture kept him hard at work. As his first commissioned piece, it depicted the faces of a family of four. The blown up photograph was taped to the wall behind the image he currently worked on, a five-by-six sculpture in relief. He stood in front of it, carving the lines of hair into the little boy's head.

Samirah rubbed his back.

"Did he get out of here on time?"

"Yeah, I think he made it. Barely." She kissed his shoulder blade. "Did you sleep down here last night?"

"Yes, I didn't want to disturb you by coming in and leaving again after a few hours, so I slept on the sofa. I wanted to get as much done as possible. They put down a large deposit and are paying a high price for a fast turnaround, and I don't want to miss the deadline."

"You need to get some rest."

"I know. I appreciate all your help with him." He turned to her, tired lines around his mouth. "What are you doing today?"

"In a little bit I'm going next door to have coffee with Geneva and Thomas. Then I'm going into town to drop off resumes and fill out more applications. I wish that one bakery off Parque Calderon would call me. I'd love to work there."

"Don't worry, you'll find something."

He dropped the scraper onto the table with the other tools. "I think I will take a nap. I'm tired." He smothered a yawn. "How about I meet you for lunch?"

"Sounds good."

"And ah...could you do me a favor? I have a friend who leased a space in town, right off the park. It used to be a restaurant. The previous owners abandoned it to return overseas, and he wants to open another restaurant in the same spot. I'll take you to look at it, and I want you to tell me what you think."

"Sure. Which friend is it?" She wasn't aware any of his friends were interested in opening a restaurant. Maybe she could find work there.

"No one you know." He walked over to the sink to wash up. "I'll see you later, okay?"

"Okay."

* * *

SAMIRAH SAT in a shaded spot on the grass in Parque Calderon with an empty container that had previously contained roasted pork and potato cakes. She'd been so hungry she wolfed it down.

The park was a popular hang out in town. It was filled with

palm trees and benches and a well-tended lawn. Cafes and other businesses surrounded it, tucked into colonial-style buildings. From here she could see one of the city's main attractions, the New Cathedral of Cuenca. Three domes covered in sky blue tile sat atop the Romanesque-style building across the street.

People bustled by, an interesting blend of old and new. Some wore trendy, cosmopolitan clothing with cell phones glued to their ears. Meanwhile, several indigenous women strolled past in their colorful skirts holding the hands of their little ones with babies strapped to their backs in blankets. A man leading a small herd of goats offered fresh milk for sale.

Reclining on one elbow, Miguel stirred beside her. He was almost finished with his food. He'd purchased a couple of *humitas*, a tamale-like dish made of corn, onions, cheese, and spices wrapped in a corn husk from his favorite vendor. The scent of it wafted over to Samirah and stoked her appetite even though she'd already finished her own meal.

"Have some." He must be a mind reader. He lifted a forkful of the fragrant dish toward her mouth. Although full, the tantalizing aroma induced her to part her lips and partake. The savory flavor of the cheese and spices intermingled with the fresh vegetables exploded across her palate, forcing out a soft moan.

"Good, no?"

She nodded, chewing slowly. "Heaven on a fork."

"Have some more."

She shook her head in protest. "No, I shouldn't. Are you trying to fatten me up?"

"No, but I like to watch you eat."

"You like to watch me do anything," she said, leaning forward to kiss him.

"True," he murmured against her mouth. "Especially one of your strip teases."

"Oh, you really like that."

He laughed as he finished his meal. "One day I'll get you to try *cuy*."

Samirah shook her head. She couldn't imagine eating guinea pig, especially since the custom in Ecuador was to roast them or fry them whole—head, paws, and all.

"How about if I cut off the head for you so it doesn't seem so strange?"

"How about no? I'm an adventurous eater, but I don't care what you do, I'm not eating that." She made a face.

Miguel laughed and rose to his feet. He reached down to help her up.

"Okay, let me show you the place I told you about."

They strolled across the street hand in hand and he let them into the building. "Wow, this is nice," Samirah said. Her eyes roamed over the high ceilings and the little round tables set up around the room. "Small, but nice."

"They left all of this," Miguel said. "The new owner bought the furniture, appliances, and everything in here at a good price."

"Who did you say leased this place?"

"There's a little courtyard in the back, too, for extra seating." He led the way out the glass doors to the exterior.

"Nice. Extra tables could be set up out here for sure. They could even rent this out for private parties because it's completely enclosed by the buildings around it."

They walked back inside and she checked out the kitchen with Miguel following silently behind. Whoever owned the restaurant before must not have stayed long or they were extremely careful. The kitchen showed some wear and tear, but overall it was in good condition.

Back in the main part of the restaurant, she placed her hands on her hips and scanned the room. "This is nice. Your friend is lucky. There's not much work to be done in here, and they have a prime spot off Parque Calderon, too."

A little bit of envy twisted inside her. She would have to adjust her sketches, but if this were her place, she could work some magic. A takeout counter could be added over there, and bright colors would spruce the place up. Maybe orange…no, too much…a soft green, or an aqua blue.

"So you like it?" Miguel asked, a curious tone to his voice.

"In my opinion, it's a good investment."

"In that case, it's yours."

He spoke so quietly, she almost didn't hear him. She took a good look at him. His features had tightened, and she noted the tension in his broad shoulders. "Wh-what do you mean it's mine?"

"What's the matter with your English? Do you need me to spell it out for you?" he teased.

"Miguel, I can't accept this. It's too much." Had those words actually come from her mouth? She was turning down her dream. "It's nice of you to do, but we're still…I mean…this isn't a gift you give your girlfriend."

"You're not just my girlfriend. We live together."

"I know, but…" She struggled to find the right words. "We don't really, really know this is permanent, do we?"

Frown lines marred his forehead. "What are you saying? You plan to leave me?"

"No, I'm only trying to… I love you for doing this, but it doesn't feel right. I can't."

"Will you accept my gift if you're my wife?"

Samirah's mouth fell open. "Are you asking me?" Her heart thudded against her breastbone.

"It's not the way I planned it. Nothing ever goes the way I plan with you. There were supposed to be rose petals and champagne, and a ring." He raked his fingers through his hair, the increased tension in him obvious. "It's small, it's not your dream, it's not South Beach. But do you think you could stay here, in this small place, and be happy? Could you be happy as my wife? Could you...?" The words rushed out of him, his accent thickening. "Could you stay for good? Maybe during the slow season we could close the restaurant and you could take me to see some of those places you've been to, and we could visit a few for the first time together."

"Say it," Samirah said in a choked voice. "Ask me."

He looked intently at her, and she saw the love there. "Will you marry me?"

His image blurred before her eyes, and she couldn't speak. All she managed was a nod.

"I can't believe I've finally found a way to shut you up."

She laughed, tears of happiness flowing down her cheeks. "It's temporary, so enjoy it while you can." She brushed the tears away. "Yes," she said. "Yes! Yes! *Si! Oui! Sim!* Yes!"

She ran and jumped into his arms. He stumbled backward, but he was strong, bracing his body and maintaining his balance before they toppled backwards.

"What would you have done if I'd hated it?"

He chuckled softly. As always, the sound was so inviting and sensual it sent warm ripples through her belly. "I don't know. I would have been stuck with a lease on a property I couldn't use." He squeezed her tight. "Samirah, Samirah," he whispered. "I love you."

She covered his face in kisses. "I love you, too, Miguel. I'll always love you. Always."

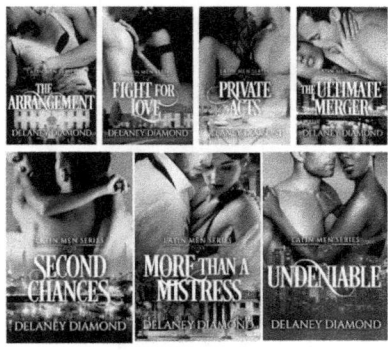

Check out the entire Latin Men series with heroes from Mexico, Ecuador, Brazil, and Argentina: The Arrangement, Fight for Love, Private Acts, The Ultimate Merger, Second Chances, More Than a Mistress, and Undeniable.

ABOUT THE AUTHOR

Delaney Diamond is the USA Today Bestselling Author of sweet, sensual, passionate romance novels. Originally from the U.S. Virgin Islands, she now lives in Atlanta, Georgia. She reads romance novels, mysteries, thrillers, and a fair amount of nonfiction. When she's not busy reading or writing, she's in the kitchen trying out new recipes, dining at one of her favorite restaurants, or traveling to an interesting locale.

Enjoy free reads on her website. Join her mailing list to get sneak peeks, notices of sale prices, and find out about new releases.

Join her mailing list
www.delaneydiamond.com

- facebook.com/DelaneyDiamond
- twitter.com/DelaneyDiamond
- bookbub.com/authors/delaney-diamond
- pinterest.com/delaneydiamond